The Devil's Gospel

by

A.S. Coomer

The Devil's Gospel

COPYRIGHT © 2019 by A.S. Coomer

Cover Art by *Kristian Norris*

The Wild Rose Press, Inc.
PO Box 708
Adams Basin, NY 14410-0708
Visit us at www.thewildrosepress.com

Publishing History
First Crimson Rose Edition, 2019
Print ISBN 978-1-5092-2159-2
Digital ISBN 978-1-5092-2160-8

Published in the United States of America

The storm broke before Evelyn could put any of the windows up. She had them open on account of the warmer weather. The spring was finally showing and with it the unexpected heavy thunderstorms she used to be so scared of when she was younger. She hurried about the first floor slamming windows shut and sliding on the already wet hardwood.

She closed both deck doors and raced upstairs as the storm raged into culmination. It looked like a broken faucet the way water was streaming into the house, soaking the carpets. She'd just had them cleaned, too.

"Stupid, fickle woman," she called herself.

All the windows closed, she set about soaking up the water from the carpets. She laid out thick bath towels under the windows and on her hands and knees pressed and pressed. She moved back downstairs and wrapped bath towels around her feet and scooted across the slippery hardwood.

The thunderous roar of the storm had settled into a kind of grumbling, like great sleeping beasts rested just outside the windows in the steaming fog. She had just dropped the last wet towel into the hamper when the lights cut out. She stood straight up and groped about blindly with her hands for something to steady herself on. She found the dresser and held onto it with both hands while squinting into the inky, hot darkness. She forced herself to slow her breathing but couldn't help feeling that childish fright with each flash of lightning and rumble of thunder.

Dedication

For David, Ethan, Rachel, and Sherry Coomer,
with special thanks to
Juanita Wigginton, S.L. Kerns, Aaron Hawkins,
and Vivian Baumgardner

Chapter One

The storm broke before Evelyn could put any of the windows up. She had them open on account of the warmer weather. The spring was finally showing and, with it, the unexpected heavy thunderstorms she used to be so scared of when she was younger. She hurried about the first floor, slamming windows shut and sliding on the already wet hardwood.

She closed both deck doors and raced upstairs as the storm raged into culmination. It looked like a broken faucet, the way water was streaming into the house, soaking the carpets. She'd just had them cleaned, too.

"Stupid, fickle woman," she called herself.

After closing all the windows, she set about soaking up the water from the carpets. She laid out thick bath towels under the windows and, on her hands and knees, pressed and pressed. She moved back downstairs and wrapped bath towels around her feet and scooted across the slippery hardwood.

The thunderous roar of the storm had settled into a kind of grumbling, like great sleeping beasts rested just outside the windows in the steaming fog. She had just dropped the last wet towel into the hamper when the lights cut out. She stood straight up and groped about blindly with her hands for something to steady herself on. She found the dresser and held onto it with both hands while squinting into the inky, hot darkness. She forced herself to slow her breathing but couldn't help feeling that childish fright with each flash of lightning and rumble of thunder.

She made it down the narrow hall, her hand sliding down across the wall, keeping her path straight in the dark, looking out the window with a fear she didn't want to acknowledge.

A soundless lightning strike illuminated the empty, wet county road out front. The wall she was guiding herself with ended. She crossed the mudroom into the kitchen slowly, just able to make out the shapes of the walls. She couldn't recall it ever being this dark before. Not since she was a little girl. And most nights seemed as dark as dark could be.

She tried the kitchen light switch before she could catch herself; some things were just reflex. She cursed herself under her breath and felt her way around the kitchen to the cabinet with the flashlight. She switched it on, and it flickered to life, coppery and weak. She crossed the kitchen back to the mudroom, opened a drawer of the cupboard, and got out the matches and tealight candles. She lit the candles one by one and set them on tables, cabinets, and desks about the first floor.

The thunder bellowed loudly, the beasts threatening to unleash the full din of the storm upon the old house again.

She winced at the lightning strike so near to the house and dropped the flashlight. Just outside the window, in the front yard, it seemed. The flashlight had gone out, so she reached down to pick it up. She flicked the switch several times, still crouched on her haunches, her aged knees and ankles creaking. The flashlight wouldn't come back on.

"Fickle, clumsy old git," she cussed herself.

She took the broken flashlight in one hand and set the other on her knee and heaved herself back to her feet.

Lightning flashed out front. A tall, slender dark shape just off the front porch flickered in the strike's incandescence.

"Lord Jesus," she cried and dropped the flashlight again. It fell, crushing her bare toes. She swore and fell to her knees, rubbing the smarting foot and toes.

Thunder growled, soft and low.

"Lord Jesus." That had been the shape of a man, she was sure of it. A towering man at that.

She climbed to one foot slowly, peeking over the trinket-filled windowsill onto the front porch and out into the steaming front yard. She couldn't make out the front porch posts from the trees. It was too dark. Maybe she hadn't seen anything; her imagination turning over rocks and making snakes out of little worms. She climbed all the way to her feet and made her way back to the kitchen, using the dim tealights. She shuffled through the junk drawer, looked for batteries, but didn't find any. She lit more tealights and lined them up on the kitchen counter as if they held some sort of magic, some restoring remedy or warding spell, whispering to herself, "Lord Jesus."

Her cell phone. She saw it flash in her mind like another lightning strike and realized she had left it in the cup holder of the car. Outside. Across the front yard to the driveway. She cussed Jim, ten years dead, for not letting her build on a garage like she had wanted and instantly felt guilty.

She had pulled another match from the box and was getting ready to strike it when she heard the creak of one of the deck doors. She'd closed them. One was open or opening.

"Lord Jesus." She trembled, dropping the match.

****

Turning off 65 at the Sonora exit, Kevin pulled up to the pump and did his best to rub the sleep from his eyes. He killed the engine and stepped out into the fog, under the florescent lights, and stretched.

It had been a long drive, the first half of which had been through the winding hills of eastern Kentucky in the driving rain. He'd even had to pull over, somewhere on the Bluegrass Parkway between Lexington and Bardstown, for the first time since he was sixteen and just learning how to drive.

He twisted off his gas cap and stuck the nozzle of the hose in. He flicked the handle twice, but nothing came out. He turned back to the pump and hit the button for unleaded, then tried the handle again. Nothing. Becoming frustrated, he turned back to the pump. A small, handwritten sign read: Please Pay Before Pumping. Thanks, Mgmt.

It had only been a couple of months since Kevin had been back this way. He'd stopped at that very gas station dozens of times over the years. Stopped, put the nozzle in, filled up, and walked in to get a cherry cola from the fountain before paying and hitting the road. Now he had to pay before he pumped. Ridiculous. Nobody trusted nobody. Couldn't even save a man a trip. He'd have to walk inside, give the attendant two twenties because he didn't know exactly how much it would be to fill up, walk back to the pump to fill up,

4

then walk back inside to get his cherry soda, and retrieve his change from the cashier before walking back to his car and leaving. And he had another half-hour of driving in front of him.

"Goddamnit," he cussed, walking across the parking lot into the gas station.

****

Everything stopped, save the candlelight flickering. She stood erect and very still, listening. The thunder had died away. The lightning hadn't flashed for several seconds. Seconds that felt as long as years.

She had shut the deck doors, both of them. She was sure of it. She had shut them while closing all the windows before racing upstairs to close the windows up there. But there was no mistaking that sound. The squeaking of the deck door on the far side of the living room that opened onto the uncovered deck, the stairs descending to the backyard, and the Nolin River. She'd meant to spray a lubricate on that damn door for years but kept putting it off. Jim would've done it eventually had he not up and died.

"Oh, Jim," she whispered. His name still made her stomach knot, made her almost forget about the squeaking deck door, until she heard it again.

"Lord Jesus," she said and opened the silverware drawer for a knife.

****

Read the sign, dumbass, Angela thought, watching the tall man outside squeeze the pump handle over and over again. She watched the man turn back to the pump and savagely jab the unleaded button with his pointer finger.

Ding. Ding.

Her cell phone. She scooped it off the counter.

When do u git off? asked the text from Brian.

11:30 pm and it's bin really ded 2nite, her response. She hit the green send button just as the bells on the front door clanged together.

The tall man walked over to the fountain machine and filled a 32-ounce MegaGulp with cherry cola. She watched as he carefully put the lid on the cup, then slid in the straw.

God, he's pale.

With his back toward Angela, he brought the drink up to his mouth. The man jerked up and stood very straight. Angela thought the man may have just shit himself the way he jerked up like that and couldn't help but snicker.

The man turned around slowly, the MegaGulp in his right hand, his left reaching deep into the pocket of his black overcoat.

Angela's cell phone dinged. She picked it up and brought it before her face, instinct.

Brian: *I caint wait to c u, sweetie.*

Angela's smile broadened, and she opened the phone's keyboard to send a reply. She didn't hear the tall man approach the counter until he slammed the MegaGulp against the cash register, splashing the cherry soda everywhere.

"Jesus Christ," she swore.

****

After she lit the last candle and flipped off the lights, Kate slipped into the steaming bathtub of water she had drawn for herself. Kevin couldn't have dipped a toe in the water. It was so hot, but that was the way she liked it. Kevin had gone home to visit his mother that weekend, something he hadn't done in quite some time, she gathered. His mother, whom she had yet to meet, lived in Hardin County on her own. Kevin's father had died some years back. She'd been meaning to ask Kevin how he died, but it was such an awkward question that she never could quite steer the conversation in its direction, especially only four months into a relationship. Kevin had had some falling out with his parents before his father's death, but it was obvious that he loved his mother despite their differences and talked about her often.

Kate slid lower in the tub until the water line was just under her nose. She closed her eyes and breathed slowly. She was tired. She'd hiked every trail the Red River Gorge had to offer, at least, three times over during the last month and a half. She and Kevin had taken residence in a small cabin for the duration of the research project. They'd spent their days together hiking on and off the trails, counting white-haired goldenrod and checking out their surroundings. She snapped pictures of Canadian Yew and hemlock, which were much more beautiful in her opinion, when Kevin wasn't looking.

Kate felt the tension in her legs ease and tried not to think about the blisters on both of her feet. On Kevin's advice, she'd went out and bought an expensive pair of hiking boots, especially for that reason.

"I guess some things can't be helped," she thought out loud.

"No, they cain't," a voice behind her answered.

Kate tried to scream, but she sucked in a mouthful of bathwater and choked.

****

The knife fell from Evelyn's shaking hand, clanging uselessly onto the hardwood. The strong hands had come from behind and wrapped around her windpipe before she could suck in a last breath. Evelyn struggled against them. She flailed with her arms and legs wildly before everything went black.

****

Kevin didn't make it two steps inside the gas station before he realized something was wrong. There was a puddle of soda on the floor and a smashed styrofoam MegaGulp cup on the counter beside the cash register.

"Hello?" he called out.

No response.

Weird.

Kevin walked back to the unisex bathroom and entered. He unzipped and used the urinal. His phone vibrated in his pocket, and he used one hand to fish it out and unlock the screen. A small emoticon cross appeared, and the message was from an unknown number.

"What?" he said.

He shook his head, slid the phone back into his pocket, and washed his hands. Kevin opened the bathroom door and walked through each of the small aisles. The place seemed empty.

He walked around the puddle and leaned over the counter.

"Oh, Christ." He jumped back, sliding in the soda spill.

The amount of blood overwhelmed Kevin, and he felt his body sway. He was afraid he was going to be sick, but he couldn't look away. After he had regained his bearings, the girl's age was the next thing he noticed. She couldn't have been more than twenty years old. Even in death, she had the doe-eyed look of youth.

Kevin wrestled his cell phone out of his pocket with shaky hands. He told the 911 operator about the girl behind the counter and where they were. He told her his name, Dr. Kevin Ballard, associate professor of biology, University of Kentucky, like he was reading his CV or giving a lecture. She asked him more questions, and he found himself unable to concentrate on the call; there was just so much blood.

He knew she was dead as soon as he saw her. He didn't even think about seeing if she had a pulse or was breathing at all. What if she had been alive when he arrived and died when he was pissing? He might've saved her life.

No. That's all bullshit and he knew it.

Kevin asked the dispatcher to repeat what she had just said.

"How do you know she's dead?" the operator asked.

"I can see right down to the bone on both of her forearms. All the way down to the wrist. There's blood everywhere," Kevin said, his mouth wooden, the words difficult to form.

He stepped back over the soda spill and crossed to the fountain machine. He filled the cup with ice, then cherry soda. All the while, his phone cradled on his shoulder, the operator talking. "Sir? Sir, please remain on the line and don't leave the scene. Do not touch anything. A trooper will be there momentarily. Are you there, sir?"

"Yes, ma'am. I was getting a drink."

His phone beeped once, then died.

"Goddamnit," Kevin yelled at the blank screen.

Chapter Two

Evelyn awoke weak, beyond all weakness she had ever known. She tried to lift her head but couldn't; she didn't have the strength. She tried to move her arms but found she couldn't move them either.

Her eyes were blurry, and she couldn't make them focus.

Through the dimness of the candlelight, she came to the realization that she was lying on her dinner table. She could make out the shape of the hanging lamp above her and the window to her right.

She tried again to lift her head but could barely lift it off the table. It slid left, and her living room, albeit blurry, came into view. The tall, dark shape of a man was busy removing pictures from the wall. The man took off each picture carefully and set it on the couch. After he'd taken off the last picture, he stood erect, as if he felt her eyes on his back. The man turned around with startling quickness, and Evelyn would've jumped if she could've.

She felt the man looking at her and squinted but couldn't make out anything beyond the shadow of a man. The man crossed the room and walked to the head of the table, directly behind Evelyn's head, out of view. She could hear him breathing behind her, but all she could see when she opened her eyes was her dimly lit living room. Her eyes closed against her will. They were so heavy. She felt so tired. She fought to keep her eyes open, but it was far too much for her.

She opened her eyes once more and saw the dancing, orange glow from the tealight candles flickering in the wind from the open deck door on her living room wall. Then she saw nothing.

****

The trooper arrived not five minutes after Kevin's phone had died. Kevin was sitting in his SUV with the engine running, charging it. The trooper was young with a fresh, closely cropped crew cut. He flew out of the door of the police car, talking in a hurried voice into the shoulder-mounted radio.

Kevin killed the engine and stepped out under the florescent lights, crossing the parking lot. The trooper was already opening the glass door when Kevin called out, "Officer."

The trooper spun on his heels, his hand resting on the butt of his gun.

Kevin immediately recognized the state trooper as Derrick Bohannon. They'd both graduated from Central Hardin High School, just down the interstate, in Elizabethtown.

"Derrick? Derrick Bohannon?" Kevin said.

"Ballard. Jesus. What's happened?"

"I don't know. Tried to gas up, but the sign said I had to pay first, so I went in. Nobody was in there, but then I saw that broken cup and the spill and thought somebody must've went to the back to get the mop to clean it up or something. I took a leak, and when I came back out, the spill was still there, but I didn't see anybody around. I looked over the counter and saw her there. Jesus, there's so much blood," Kevin said, unable to control the fear in his throat.

Trooper Bohannon nodded his head in understanding and answered some unintelligible murmur from the radio.

"You stand right here and don't move, Ballard," he said and walked through the door into the gas station.

****

Kevin tried calling his mother several times after giving Trooper Bohannon his statement and speaking with a few other troopers, paramedics, and firemen. She didn't answer her cell phone, and the home phone wouldn't even ring. It just beeped like it was busy or unplugged.

The relatively short drive from the gas station to his mother's house, about twenty-five minutes, seemed longer. Kevin couldn't help but see all the blood and the girl's young face in his head. He turned the radio over to AM to listen to someone, anyone talk. It was all a lot of static. He hit the scan button and called Kate. She didn't answer either, but that was to be expected; cellphone reception in Red River Gorge was spotty at best. He thought about leaving her a message but decided against it. He'd send her a text when he got to his mother's house.

Darkened farmland whirled by the windows. Kevin found an AM station call-in show discussing Kentucky basketball, a regional religion almost, and hit the scan button again to stay on the station.

"Like I said all season, Matt, 'you just gotta lettum play.' They's all All-Americans, by God. 'Lettum play's' what I said and look what happened," an older man's voice declared, tremulous and frail but triumphant.

"I think you about hit the nail on the head there, Earl. We appreciate ya calling. Take care. All right, the next thing we're gonna talk about is next season's crop. Calipari has done it again, and we'll tell you how when we come back," the voice was quick, magisterial.

There were pinholes of brightness in the night just ahead. Kevin Ballard braked just before St. Ignatius, letting seven deer cross from the stygian steeple and darksome tree line into the open field on the other side. He watched each jump the fence gracefully and disappear into the night.

****

He'd brought another clipping of an article he'd written over a year ago that finally made it to print. He'd forgotten all about it until the wind from the open windows scuffled it around. It was in a manila folder sitting on the passenger side seat. He reached back, grabbed his small duffle bag, filled with some shorts, a change of clothes, his medications, and his toothbrush, and set it on the folder to keep it from blowing out the window. He didn't want to roll them up; he needed the air.

He'd have to slip in quietly. He didn't see much use in waking his mother in the middle of the night, getting her all riled up with the outrageous situation he'd just experienced in little ol' Sonora. Hopefully they'd keep his name out of the papers, say a motorist found such-and-such. Not Dr. Kevin Ballard, University of Kentucky evolutionary biologist, found such-and-such gutted and left for dead in a gas station in hick-ass Sonora.

No, he hoped to sneak into the house with his key, if he needed it—she didn't lock the doors most of the time—and climb the stairs quietly to his old bedroom and sleep without dreams.

Lord!

As tired as he was, he hadn't thought of actually sleeping until that point. He'd be lying tonight in a bed that, although it used to be his, he hadn't slept in for years. He'd have to sleep there in what was now almost a stranger's environment with all that blood sitting right in the forefront of his memory.

"Great," he said, "just fucking great."

Kevin turned off 84, onto his parents' road.

"Mom's road," he corrected himself.

Dad has been dead almost ten years now. How strange that thought felt. Sure, it was a part of life, but no one truly accepts the fact that, God willing and the creek don't rise, you would see the death of, at least, one but, more than likely, both of your parents. *God willing and the creek don't rise.* An expression his dad had used and used frequently.

All these ruminations on death. Such a strange, strange night. At least, it's almost over, he thought.

The clock on the dashboard read 12:30 am, and Kevin was tired.

****

Kevin noticed the porch lights weren't on. She always left the porch lights on when she knew he was coming to visit. He pulled into the gravel driveway slowly, trying to be as quiet as possible. His mother had always been a light sleeper, a trait she'd passed on to Kevin. He shut the car door softly and walked across the stepping stone pathway, onto the front porch.

The house was lit but very dimly. Through the frosted glass of the front door, candlelight flickered in the living room. Kevin unlocked the door and pushed it in gently. He held the door knob until he shut the door and released it quietly. Kevin then turned around and walked across the mudroom, into the living room. He tried the mudroom light switch, but it didn't work.

A neat stack of picture frames sat on the green floral-printed couch. Walking toward them, he crossed the living room but stopped short when he saw the kitchen table.

****

His mother lay on her kitchen table, surrounded by tealight candles. Kevin approached the table slowly, as if she were only sleeping, and he didn't want to wake her. His foot squished into a coagulating puddle of blood that had dripped off onto the hardwood floor.

"Oh, Christ," he whispered.

A rush of wind fluttered the candlelight, and the deck door bounced off the doorstop; it was wide open. The sliding screen door was shut only partially, and a pair of leaves from the flowering dogwood skittered across the floor, then stuck in the semisolid blood like flies in sap.

For the second time that night, Kevin found himself surprised at how much blood could pour from a human body. The tealights stuck out like little islands in a tenebrific crimson sea. He felt detached, like he was someone completely unrelated to the person lying before him. A person that was familiar with the sight of the dead.

There was a cross on his mother's forehead extending down the bridge of her nose, the arms of which matted down her normally bushy eyebrows. It had been finger-painted in her own blood. There were blood smears on her cheeks, resembling watercolor hands, like some claret aunt had squeezed her face and welcomed her to hell.

Another gust of wind swept through the open door and carried in a few more discarded dogwood leaves, and with it, a chill ran the length of Kevin's spine. He lifted his foot from the mess with a suction pop and watched the viscid mass settle back onto the floor.

He slid the phone out of his pocket and dialed 911 for the second time that night.

****

White Mills, to many, was not a city. It was not even a town. Its residents lived here and there, sometimes with miles in between them, long, empty miles at that. The space was a comfort. Folks liked their neighbors, sure, but neighbors were best over there. Over here was where you lived. Where your family took care of the things that needed taking care of. Where, sometimes, it might just feel like you were alone.

It took the police nearly twenty minutes to respond to Kevin's call.

He paced around the kitchen table and his mother's body like a panther in a zoo. His first couple of laps eased a fraction of his anxiety. He looked around, at the pictures on the couch, the blood on the table, the floor, the carpet, and the wall.

The wall read: *Repent, Sinner*.

Written in Evelyn Ballard's blood by very large hands.

Kevin couldn't help but think of the turkey hand paintings every school-aged child in the United States slapped together before Thanksgiving. He remembered making them for his parents.

The man had smeared great gobs of his mother's blood on the wall and had written his message with one large, thin finger.

Repent, Sinner.

Kevin didn't understand. His mother was a self-professed "deeply spiritual woman," whatever that meant. She'd believed in God and had tried to convince him to believe as well. They had almost come to rows several times when she just wouldn't let it rest.

"I'm afraid for your soul, Kevin," she'd say, all teary eyed and motherly.

He'd told her that this soul she spoke of didn't exist. There was no proof of it. Then she'd taken a line straight from the gleaming teeth of her favorite multi-millionaire televangelist. "What does your heart tell you, Kevin? Listen to your heart."

That had hurt. Not because he feared eternal damnation in sorrow and agony. It hurt because he could tell she really believed it. She was completely invested in something as ludicrous as the fairies in the lilies, trolls under bridges, or the white unicorn galloping in secret.

Repent, Sinner.

"Christ," he swore. Who would be sick enough to do something like this but a wingnut Christian?

Kevin crossed the living room, into the kitchen. He pulled down the bottle of bourbon that had been in the cabinet above the stove years before his father's death. He unscrewed the lid and took a swig from the bottle. He didn't even feel it go down.

Kevin walked back to the kitchen table and cringed when he realized the body looked less and less like his mother with each glance. He slammed the deck door without meaning to, then walked back into the kitchen and took another hit of bourbon.

He slid his cell phone out of his pants pocket and tried Kate again. It rang all the way through to voicemail, and this time, he left her one. "Kate. It's me. I need you to call me back. Please."

He slid the phone back into his pocket and tried the light switch again.

Angry at the lights, like they'd caused this mess, he stomped down the long hall to the fuse box. He flipped each one to no avail. He stepped back to the front door and looked out the window toward the Randalls' house, some two hundred yards back up the road. Their security light shined yellow in the darkness.

Kevin walked back to the fuse box and flipped the switches again. Still no result.

He turned around and found himself at the foot of the stairs to the second floor. His old bedroom was up there, as well as the guest bedroom, a bathroom, and a dormer room that his mother used as an office.

He tried the light. *Stupid*. How many times was he going to keep doing that?

Kevin walked back into the kitchen and opened the cabinet where his parents kept the flashlight and other junk. He didn't see the big, old, plastic flashlight that they'd had since he was a kid. He found a small keychain penlight, however, and it worked. He turned to leave the kitchen and see what monstrosity lurked upstairs for him and saw the old flashlight sitting on the counter, not two feet from the bottle of bourbon he had just set down. He hadn't noticed it earlier.

He picked it up, heard the small bulb clink inside.

He tried the switch anyway and confirmed that it was busted. He set it back on the counter and considered another hit of bourbon but decided against it. The last shot sat on his sternum like heartburn.

****

Kevin used the penlight to lead himself up to the landing. Its light was small and weak. He slid his cell phone out of his pocket and used the camera's flash instead. He walked up the other half of the stairs and scanned the open dormer room. No bloody messages on the walls. Nothing out of the ordinary that he could tell.

He passed through the open guest room door. The oversized bed was made with extra pillows and quilts. He walked around the room and checked the closet. Nothing. He fell to his knees and checked under the bed. Again, nothing.

Kevin crossed the dormer to the bathroom and shined in his light. He caught a glimpse of himself in the mirror, a pale, drawn face partially obscured by the bright white LED light of the cell phone. He remembered whispering "Bloody Mary" over and over again into the mirror with his friends. That seemed so long ago now.

He moved down the short hall to his bedroom. The door was shut. He switched the cell phone to his left hand and grabbed the doorknob with his right, but it slipped. He jerked his hand away and nearly dropped the cell phone. He turned the camera around and held his right hand to the light. A thick glob of blood sloshed off his fingertips, onto the small light, temporarily leaving him in the red-tinged dark.

A flicker of light shined under the door.

Kevin wiped the phone against his jeans and turned

the light back to the door and used his shirt tail to open it. He had expected to find his mother's murderer sitting on his bed. Some masked madman, Michael Myers-like and waiting.

He didn't.

Chapter Three

"I think the real issue is ignorance," Kevin said, wiping sweat from his eyes.

"Ignorance? I think you might have just stumbled onto the greatest understatement in the history of the great Commonwealth of Kentucky." Kate laughed.

"How so?" Kevin asked.

"There's an unmistakable pride in ignorance in some of these people, Kev. They don't know, and they don't *want* to know. They're proud to be ignorant. Jesus, that's not coming out right," Kate said, stepping over a dead, fallen tree in the trail. "What I mean is, it's almost like they want to believe they're innocent because they don't know how a lot of things actually work. Like, by learning something, their whole, beautiful fantasy world would come screaming to a halt. Like, by attempting to educate, we are insulting their way of life and then their Jesus Christ or John Smith or who-the-fuck-ever would come crashing down with hammers and swords a'swinging, if they did nothing less than beat their puffed chests and scream, 'No! I will not listen to your sacrilege!'" Kate laughed, lightly thumping her chest with both fists.

Kevin laughed along with her.

"I remember this girl sitting at the table in front of me in my Intro to Geology lab in undergraduate on the first day. The professor walks in, this old, bearded grumpy Gus, and tells the class that the earth is approximately four point five-four billion years old. That girl's head snapped to the side like a dog trying to hear better or understand something. The professor must've caught the girl's expression, too, because he walked over to that table and said, 'Yes, four point five-four billion years old.'

"Then he walked over to the wall and opened a cabinet and brought out a glass-lidded box with several rocks in it. He took it over to that table with the girl— she was blonde, by the way—and set it on the table. He pointed at a rock and said, 'This one, Corbin Sandstone, is somewhere in the ballpark of 307 to 325 Ma, meaning Mega Annum or millions of years ago, and can be found all over the Red River Gorge area.'

"He saw an expression on that girl's face that he must've enjoyed because he set that rock back in the box and pulled out another. He held it up and said, 'This limestone was from the Slade Formation in the Mississippian subsystem and was somewhere close to 315 to 330 Ma and also found in the eastern Kentucky region,'" Kate reenacted in her best Socrates interrogation and sorority consternation, stoically serious, then comically shocked, respectively.

"That girl pushed herself back from the table and was on her feet so fast the professor didn't have time to hide the shock from his face. She was up, leaning across the table, pointing a finger under his nose, yelling, 'Lies! All of it! Earth ain't but six-thousand years old. Good Book says so.' Then she stormed out of the classroom, and she didn't come back. That was on the first day. The first day!" Kate laughed.

Kevin loved her laugh. It was easy and musical, a

bird's song almost. They walked on down the trail for a minute in silence, Kevin waiting to see if Kate was going to add anything else, but she didn't.

"I don't necessarily mean ignorance like that. I'm talking about telling the people, listen, this plant right *here*," Kevin said and held his hand up, holding the invisible plant. "This plant right here is globally imperiled. That means it's almost extinct, kaput, gone, lost, so we need to be sure we don't crush it, pick it, or destroy its habitat," Kevin said.

He let his hand fall, the invisible plant, invisibly falling onto the dirt trail to wither and die.

"I don't think you fully appreciate the power of the redneck's pride. I think, if we came around the corner just now and came upon Jimmy Bob stomping all over some dago albo and you ran over and said, 'Jimmy Bob, hey, would you cut it out? This plant right *here*…'" Kate, too, lifted the invisible squashed plant. "'This plant right here is very rare. And this is the only place in the world it grows. I think we all gotta pitch in and make sure nothing bad happens to it, so it doesn't go extinct.' I think, aside from the ass whipping you most surely would catch, you would probably get an asshole full of smashed *Solidago albopilosa*, as well," Kate said, laughing.

Kevin loved that she was always laughing.

****

Kevin took a bite from the sandwich and stared at the chips on his plate. The silence was awkward and uncomfortable, but he resigned to hold onto it, if it kept him from this discussion again.

"I know what you're thinking," Jim Ballard told his son. "You're thinking that old-fashioned Dad is behind the times. Dad can't help that he's a superstitious, old kook."

He was right, but Kevin did not acknowledge this outwardly. He took another bite of the sandwich, mustard and baloney, and stared at the chips.

"Your mother and I are just scared for you. That's all. We know you're a good person, but we don't want you to spend eternity in hell because of some scientific 'proof,'" Jim Ballard said, making bunny ears with the index and middle finger of each of his hands. He winked them forward at the beginning of the word *proof*, then again after he'd said it.

Jim Ballard picked his sandwich up and took a monstrous bite, taking nearly half of it into his mouth, bulging both cheeks out.

Kevin looked up from the chips to see if his father was finished with the talk. Kevin couldn't help but smile. His dad had eaten like that as long as he could remember, filling his mouth as full as possible and slowly chewing it all. Very bovine.

His dad smiled at him, but it looked more like a grimace. Kevin could tell his dad was beating himself up on "not getting through" to his son. His dad always looked at a loss after these little talks. Since their retirement, his parents spoke of God nearly all the damn time, it seemed. During dinners, he'd catch one or both of them staring out the window, a look of pleading on their faces, as if pleading with God Himself to please just shine through and show them how to save their son from eternal damnation.

Kevin changed the subject. "I'm just about done with my thesis. I'll submit it next week to the department. Should know something in a few weeks."

To Kevin, it looked like Jim Ballard found it difficult to swallow with a mouth so full.

****

"Remember Genesis, Kev? How God made the serpent the craftiest of all the creatures? And that crafty little bastard slithered on up to naked and naive ol' Eve and duped her into eating from the tree in the center of the Garden of Eden. God made that snake and then punished it for what it did. Before Adam and Eve had even eaten the fruit, the snake was already wreaking havoc and causing man's, or should I say woman's, original sin," Kate said, carefully stepping over a small, flowering white-haired goldenrod.

"Sure. I remember Genesis and the serpent and the Tree of Conscience. I remember the snake 'came' to the woman, but after God punished it for tricking Eve, the snake 'groveled' and 'crawled,'" Kevin said, snapping photos of the plants in the shade of the rockhouse. "For some reason, that part always stuck with me. I was little when I learned it, and it might have been the first time I read something and sensed I was being led to believe something, whereas I wanted to be presented with the facts of the story and left to make my own decision. I think that snake 'groveled' and 'crawled' up to Eve before he was punished by God. If God had made him, He made him that way."

"Jesus, Kevin. Have you been reading the Bible at night when I'm sleeping?" Kate laughed. "Picture the great man of science, Dr. Kevin Ballard, sneaking out of bed late at night, to sit up by lamplight and read from the Great Book of Indoctrination: The Holy Bible."

They both laughed.

"Some things just tend to stick with you, I guess,"

Kevin said.

"Well, anyway, if that snake, made by the hand of the Almighty, I remind you, tricked Eve, made from the rib of sleeping Adam, also by the hand of the Almighty, into the so-called 'original sin,' wouldn't it be God that caused original sin?" she asked.

Dr. Kevin Ballard snapped another picture of the budding goldenrod. He looked at the picture of the flower on the camera's digital screen and noticed the stubs on the stem. He dropped to his knees for a closer look at the plant. It was missing several leaves, and it was clear they had been cut or clipped off. The stubs were moist and leaking slightly.

Kate followed Kevin's eyes. She looked at the dago albo nearest her and noticed it was missing most of its leaves. "Somebody clipped the leaves off," she said.

Kevin held the camera up to the plant and zoomed in, snapping a picture of the stub where the leaf should have been.

****

"They fill their little heads early, don't they?" Kate said, walking out of the middle school gymnasium alongside Kevin.

Kevin nodded his head but didn't say anything. Kevin opened the hatch of the SUV and put the poster board, binder, and his computer bag inside.

"Do they normally ask questions like that?" Kate asked.

Kevin started the engine and slid his seatbelt on.

"Yes, they do," he said. "Last year, when I did this talk at this very same school, an eighth grader said, 'If evolution was real, how come there aren't crocoducks?'"

Kate laughed but Kevin didn't join her. He felt tired and grumpy after spending the last hour and a half talking about evolution and natural selection to a gym full of middle schoolers, which was a condition of a grant he'd applied for and received.

They drove the fifteen minutes back to campus in silence.

Kevin found a small package in his mailbox in the biology department. He took it inside his office, opened it, and burst into laughter.

Kate walked inside his office with raised eyebrows. "What's so funny?"

It took Kevin several moments to compose himself. "I forgot I ordered you this. It had been on backorder for weeks. What a perfect day for it to arrive, right?" Kevin said, shoving the box across the desk to Kate.

Kate picked it up. Inside was a thin gold chain necklace and attached was a small pendant of a green animal she'd never seen before.

"What?" Kate asked, sending Kevin into more laughter.

"It's an orangumantis," Kevin said, gasping in between snorts. "It's a mix between an orangutan and a praying mantis."

Kate took the necklace from the box and held it up to her face for a closer examination. It had the head of an orangutan with the eyes of a praying mantis. The animal's body was hairy and had nipples like an orangutan but was thin and elongated with the praying arms of a mantis.

Kate looked up from the orangumantis at Kevin and cracked up.

****

"Kate, come here," Kevin called from behind the two monitors.

"What's up?" She walked around his desk and propped herself up on the back of his chair.

"I just got an email from the dean about the dago albo research proposal," Kevin said.

"And?" Kate asked, squinting her eyes at the email on the right screen, reading.

"We're approved," Kevin said and craned his head over his shoulder, smiling up at Kate. She returned the smile after finishing the email and kissed the top of his head.

"Red River Gorgeous, here we come," Kate said and laughed.

****

"These have been cut, too," Kevin said, sliding his finger down the coarse white hairs of the goldenrod stem, across the clipped nub where the spade-shaped leaf should have been.

"This is so weird. This is the third group we've seen cut. If this was a cable drama, I'd say somebody was leaving us a message," Kate said and laughed, although not as carefree as she usually sounded.

"And just what would that message be?" Kevin asked.

"I don't know. These are *our* plants? Or something like that," Kate said, shaking her head.

"Or maybe the plants are cutting their own leaves off. Maybe dago albo is offering itself up to Lord Jesus to save the souls of all these heathen scientists?" Kevin laughed, pulling Kate in and embracing her. He kissed her, and they laughed together under the overhanging rock shelter.

Their laughter echoed off the rock wall and filled both of them with an unease they refused to acknowledge outwardly.

****

"*Solidago albopilosa* only exists, as far as anybody can tell, in the Red River Gorge area. We call that endemic, meaning the plant is localized or peculiar to only one place. NatureServe lists the plant as G2 Imperiled. That is only a hop-skip-and-jump away from extinct," Kevin said into the microphone, his voice sounding out of the loudspeakers, onto the audience in the small lecture hall.

"We need to do whatever we can to keep this small, delicate flowering plant from disappearing into extinction. It's a powerful piece of heritage to claim that this beautiful, little plant only exists in our state and only in our state's most beautiful park. We should take pride in this and do whatever we can to ensure its survival. In short, I plan on tracing back the plant's origins as far as I can, compiling an updated count of the species, including old and hopefully new occurrences, and seeing what can be done to minimize damage to the plant itself, as well as its environment. Thank you," Kevin said.

He scooped up his lecture notes and nodded once to the small, clapping audience and left.

Kate met him at the bottom of the stage's stairs.

"Great talk, doc!" She planted a kiss on his cheek. "Ew. You're sweating," she said through puckered lips.

"I know it. These lectures still freak me out. In the classroom, it's not so bad. You're standing at the same level as the students, don't have to use a microphone.

It's more informal and comfortable," Kevin said, using the sleeve of his shirt to mop the moisture off his forehead and the back of his neck.

"Scaredy cat, are we? The published professor prefers his dark, messy, secluded office over the bright lights of the auditorium, does he?" Kate smiled as they walked down the hall toward the biology department.

"To tell you the truth, I'd prefer to be out in the secluded woods over any of it."

"Well, we don't have to wait much longer for that. When will all the paperwork be finished?" Kate asked.

"Lord knows," Kevin said, shaking his head. "You know how it goes. The papers have to be signed by the right people, in the right time frame, and in the right order before making the rounds again. I'd say we'll be all set in a few months. I don't see the Great Shuffling of the Papers taking longer than that. Hopefully we'll catch the end of the blooming, but even if we don't, we can still work on the population count and environmental analysis."

"I can't wait." Kate smiled and kissed Kevin again before heading off to teach her 114 lab.

****

The Red Tin Cabin, despite its name, had a green, vertical paneled aluminum roof with a stone foundation and cedar siding, both inside and out. Technically it had three stories. On the first floor, there was the living room, kitchen, dining room, and bathroom. The second floor was a loft that was used as the cabin's sole bedroom. Walk up the steep cedar stairs, and there was the bed, two nightstands with lamps, and a small but crammed bookshelf. There also a railing to keep you from walking off the loft and falling onto the dinner table.

The Red Tin Cabin also had an unfinished basement. That was what the real estate lady called it. An unfinished basement. Kate could tell from looking at it that they never intended on finishing the unfinished basement, and in its incompleteness, it was actually complete.

Her grandparents had a basement just like it in their summer house out on Nolin Lake. She used to spend every summer there with Grandma and Grandpa while her parents went traveling. She hated that basement. The floor was partially concreted but eventually gave way to the dirt and rocks of the hillside the cabin was built upon. She'd have to go down there to get the floats and skis. She always felt like she'd see some pale white woman crawl out of that dungeon dirt and grab her.

Kate tried the Wi-Fi twice on her phone before bringing it up with Joan, the real estate lady.

"It's important that we have an Internet connection out here. I see the unsecured Wi-Fi network, but it doesn't work," Kate said, holding her phone out for Joan to see.

"It's spotty at best 'round here. Seems like it comes and goes. That's the best you're gonna get. Sorry," Joan said, shaking her head slightly. She smiled her big, natural smile, and Kate couldn't help but return it.

"Ok. That's about my only concern. Oh, wait. Bears. Do we have to worry about bears or cougars or anything like that over here?" Kate asked.

"Not really. There are a few bears in these parts, but they mostly keep to themselves. They mainly go for the trash cans, and you gotta drive down yonder to take the trash anyway. We got a bear-safe trash bin that you gotta pull the lever on to open. Thank the good Lord bears don't have thumbs." Joan laughed her deep, rolling laugh.

"Ok. I guess we are kind of 'out there' if we have to have a bear-proof trash can, huh? I guess we won't really need to lock our doors with bears not having thumbs and all," Kate said and laughed back.

"No, I'd lock the doors and the windows if I's y'all," Joan said.

Kate stopped laughing, but the smile remained on her face, ready to sing out again.

"You never know who's running around these hills," Joan said.

Kate stopped smiling.

****

Kinders had a small dick. Kevin caught an accidental glance of it at the urinal by the bio labs. Kevin was about halfway through pissing when Kinders called out to him. The man just walked up to the urinal and pulled his pecker out as he nodded salutations at Kevin.

"Hey, Ballard. Is the university paying for the dong bags for your 'little camping trip,' too?" Kinders made quotey fingers with the fingers of the hand that wasn't directing his flow.

Kevin didn't take the bait. He shook, washed his hands, and headed for the door, but Kinders had more to say.

"Ballard, I don't blame you. She's quite a looker. I bet she's an animal in the sack." Kinders laughed, high pitched and nasal.

Kinders was an asshole. He'd been one when they were in grad school, and he remained one now that they

33

A.S. Coomer

were both teaching. Kevin had been in the biology department for nearly nine years. Kevin was bumped up to associate professor two years ago after getting his doctoral thesis printed by the university press. Kinders very nearly got himself fired after making sexual advances toward some sorority girls in the intro bio lab he was teaching.

Kevin and Kate's relationship was the brunt of the majority of Kinders' witticisms at the moment. Kevin probably could've had Kinders canned, but he wasn't that kind of guy.

As the door closed, Kinders called out in his best Karl Childers impression, "Hope you'ns like them french fried potaters, uh huh."

****

The Red Tin Cabin was definitely off the beaten path. Kevin had turned off Route 11 onto Rogers-Glencairn Road, a small, winding road that eventually came out at Rogers Elementary School on Route 715. At Kate's direction, Kevin turned off Rogers-Glencairn Road, onto a steeply sloped, unmarked gravel path, which took them over a ridge and down the other side. They did not exceed ten miles per hour; it would have torn the car to bits if they'd gone any faster.

The drive followed Mill Creek for a-ways before cutting sharply toward it at a wide, shallow section. The drive continued on the other side. Kevin pulled up to the creek and looked over at Kate with wide eyes.

"Are you serious? A creek?" Kevin asked.

"I knew you'd love it." Kate smiled.

Kevin turned back to the creek and watched it for a bit. Then he took his foot off the brake and put it onto the gas, pulling the vehicle out into Mill Creek. Kevin held his breath the ten seconds it took to cross the small creek.

"Did you make a wish?" Kate asked.

Kevin blew out his breath. "What?" he asked.

"Did you make a wish?" she repeated. "I thought that holding your breath only applied to bridge crossing, but I'd never considered a creek, driving through one anyway."

"I hadn't even realized I was holding my breath," Kevin said.

The gravel drive climbed a ridge overlooking the confluence of Black John Creek and Mill Creek. It sloped back down and followed Black John Creek briefly before ascending, once again, to the top of the ridge where the Red Tin Cabin sat on its own.

"Jesus Christ, are we still even in the park?" Kevin asked, slowing down to pass over a deep pothole in the narrow gravel drive.

"You know I'm not even sure, but I think so. I know we're about fifteen miles away from Nada Tunnel though," Kate said, hemlocks gliding by in the passenger side window.

"How would you know?" Kevin asked her, watching her out the corner of his eyes with a Grinch-like smile climbing up his cheeks.

"All right, grumpy. If you don't believe me, you can check the map," Kate said.

"No, I mean, how do you tell whether it's a tunnel, or if it's *Nada* Tunnel? Har, har, har." Kevin mimed a hearty laugh.

"What have I gotten myself into? Sharing a cabin with the mentally disabled," Kate said, rolling her eyes, though not hiding her smile.

Chapter Four

"Chicken wire?" Kate said it like it was the gum she'd just found on her shoe.

"Well, I guess, when budgets get cut back and slashed every day, some endangered plant is going to take the cut before a congressman's private jet," Kevin said and stepped over "the fenced area," as the small sign called it.

He held the wire down for Kate.

"Watch out for the leftovers," Kevin said, nodding toward a thin sheet of ice. Small drips of water from the melting snow and ice dropped in the sandy soil under the overhang.

"I'm thoroughly sick of winter and all this cold. I can't wait to see little old dago albo sprout some pretty little flowers," Kate said.

"We've got a bit of waiting yet to do. We'll get a few weeks off in the summer for vacation. We'll try to take that sometime in the beginning to middle of August, so we'll be back for blooming. If all the hikers and climbers don't stomp it all to extinction, we're looking at a late September through the end of November bloom. Of course, all that depends on the summer…"

There was a thrashing noise coming from the far side of the rockhouse. It receded as something quickly fled into the forest.

Kevin watched the ferns and low-hanging branches sway back to stationary and listened to the loud, quick crunches of a running gait fade away into the quiet of the day.

Kevin walked under the drip line, water drops splashing onto his uncovered head and shoulders, to the fence on the far side of the rock shelter.

Another small, low-lying chicken wire fence stood at this end of the rockhouse. Just on the other side of the fence, Kevin and Kate looked at the large boot prints leading off into the hard, frozen snow and forest.

"I think we interrupted something," Kevin said.

"Either that or they were just bashful." Kate laughed but it sounded strained.

After looking out into the woods for several long moments, Kevin turned to the small cluster of white-haired goldenrod just behind him, a few steps beyond the drip line. Sitting on his haunches, Kevin examined the plants and found many of them cut, the stubs still dripping where the thin leaves should've been.

"We just missed the leaf cutter," Kevin said and showed Kate the amputated plants.

****

Kevin pulled up to the gas station pump. Kate sat in the car for a second, fixing her hair in the passenger side, pull-down mirror. She picked a bit of what appeared to be crushed leaf or bark from her hair, then pulled it back into a tight ponytail. She stepped out of the vehicle and walked around to stand with Kevin while he pumped the gas.

"Jesus Christ, you must have to prepay at every pump in the state now," he said, returning the nozzle to the pump and shaking his head.

"Don't trust the likes of you'ns around here," Kate said.

"Come on. Let's meet the local color," he said, rolling his eyes and smiling.

The sign over the door read: *The Store*.

Kate pointed up at the sign and again in her hillbilly accent said, "We's decided to call hit *the* Store on account it's the only one around these parts."

That got Kevin going. He opened the door, still laughing.

"'Cept there's one over yonder," Kate said and pointed back out the door through which they had just entered.

"Can I hep you'ns?" growled a brittle voice from behind the counter.

Kevin and Kate stopped laughing and turned toward the voice. A thin, elderly man sat on a stool behind the counter. He wore a trucker hat, just barely sitting on the top of his head. An unlit cigarette hung on his lower lip, and Kevin could see the pack in the breast pocket of his denim shirt.

Kevin cleared his throat, like he was forcing the last bit of laughing out, and said, "We're just gonna grab a few things and then fill up. Thank you, though."

"You gotta pay 'fore ye pump," the old man said.

"Yessir, I read the sign. We'll take care of that here in a second. Ok?" Kevin replied, turning and heading up one of the darkened aisles.

Kate reached out and took Kevin's hand.

"I don't think we're in Kansas anymore," she whispered, smiling up at Kevin before taking a furtive glance back toward the cash register and the watchful, beady eyes of the old man.

Kevin and Kate picked up a few candles, a long-necked lighter, a couple bags of popcorn, and a six-pack of Ale-8. They set the items on the counter in front of the old man, who just stared at Kevin for several seconds, like he was trying to see something about Kevin that seemed to shift then disappear.

"We need ten in gas, too," Kevin said.

The old man added the total up, made change for Kevin, and bagged the items. He slid the bag across the cracked counter and asked if there was anything else they'd be needing.

Wouldn't that be a question you should've asked before you rang us up? Kevin thought.

"No. No, I don't think so. Thank you, though," Kevin said and picked up the bag, ready to get the hell out of there.

"Actually, do you know much about the white-haired goldenrod?" Kate asked the old man before Kevin could even turn toward the door.

He set the bag back on the counter.

"Sure do," the old man said. "Lived here all my life. Park rangers always make a big deal out of that one. Rockhouse Goldy Rod some of 'em calls it. Not much to look at, though, in my opinion."

"Do you know of anybody around that might use the leaves for anything? Tea or art or something?" Kate asked.

Kevin smiled at her. He hadn't thought of asking anybody about the cutter. For what seemed like the millionth time over the past couple of months he found himself so glad he'd brought her along for this project.

The old man seemed to sink back and reexamine Kate and then Kevin again. They fidgeted under the scrutiny.

"What you know about them leafs?" the old man asked.

"Quite a bit, actually," Kevin said. "We're here doing some research on the plant. We're from the University of Kentucky."

The old man smiled sardonically at Kevin. He could almost read the old man's thoughts, *Well, la-dee-da*.

"Some folks around here have a different understanding of those there *leafs* than any of the stuff you'ns think ye know," the old man said. He leaned off to the side and spit dip into a waiting bucket.

"I don't follow," Kevin said, watching the long strand of phlegmy, black spit finally disconnect from the old man's paper-thin lips and fall into the bucket.

Splat.

"Course you don't. You probably ain't heard of leaf readin' either, have ye?" the old man said. It wasn't really a question.

"What in God's name are you talking about, old timer?" Kevin said.

The old man peeled out a cackling screech of a laugh.

Kate elbowed him in the ribs, hard. Kevin broke eye contact with the old man and sighed. He looked down at the bag and saw that he had goosebumps on his forearms, even though it was quite stuffy inside the Store.

"What's this leaf reading you're talking about?" Kate asked, leaning on the counter and smiling down like an old friend.

Kevin sighed but inwardly acknowledged that he

was, once again, glad Kate was with him. He probably wouldn't have learned a thing from this old man if she hadn't been there.

"Who's askin'?" the old man asked, the laugh winding down to a twisted smile, his cheeks pushed up until his eyes were nearly closed.

"I'm Kate Johnson," she said, reaching across the counter to shake the old man's hand.

The old man leaned forward off the stool and took Kate's hand gently and bent forward and kissed it. Kevin swore the old man lingered a second after and sniffed her hand.

"This is Kevin Ballard," Kate said, nodding in Kevin's direction. He forced a smile and slight nod, feeling all the while like a sullen child.

"Larry Whitaker. Pleased to meet ye, Miss Johnson," Larry Whitaker said. "I do believe I heard about some folks from the university being 'round these parts, wandering the ledges and rockhouses."

Kevin saw the ferns and low-lying branches swaying and heard the crunching footsteps of someone running away into the forest. A chill ran the length of his spine.

Before he could question him, the old man continued, "So you'ns ain't heard of leaf readin' then?"

Kevin and Kate shook their heads. No, they hadn't.

"Well, I'm not surprised. Most folks 'round *here* ain't even heard of it, and the ones that have are so old by now they probably done forgot." Larry let loose his high cackle.

They waited for the old man's laugh to die back down.

"Leaf readin's something they used to do 'fore this

became Daniel Boone National Forest or 'fore that when they called it Cumberlan' National Forest," Larry Whitaker said.

We don't need a goddamn history lesson, Kevin wanted to scream at the old man.

"See the old, old timers, myself included, knew about that there plant; what you called the 'white-hair goldy rod.' The leaf readers knowed it was only here in these parts and couldn't be found no place yonder long 'fore there were even park rangers here." Larry Whitaker motioned away from the three of them off into the darkened corner of the Store.

"How could you know that so long ago? Dr. Braun didn't discover *Solidago albopilosa* until the forties." Kevin did not hide the edge in his voice.

"Kevin," Kate said, like a mother redirecting her misbehaving child.

"You'ns think that something don't exist 'til some *doctor* writes it down in some book?" Larry Whitaker's smile was not warm.

Kevin looked off, toward the car outside by the pump, and tapped his fingers on the counter.

For the second time, Larry Whitaker looked Kevin up and down, appraising, like he was trying to measure just how much frustration Kevin was experiencing and whether or not he'd like to keep shoveling it on.

As if sensing it was enough, Larry Whitaker continued, "Called it 'White-Sight' on account it has all them little white hairs all over it and it was used in seeing through the verses."

Larry Whitaker paused, looking from Kate to Kevin and back again, appearing to be in the throes of settling some internal debate on how much they should be told about this secret history, unbeknownst to the university folk, the outsiders.

Larry Whitaker continued, "'Seeing through the verses,' they called it. See, the leaves of that there White-Sight are very thin, thin as phonebook pages, Gideon Bible pages even."

Larry Whitaker paused, his mouth working up the words like they were being manufactured by some industrial team hidden behind his thin, dry lips. He continued, "See the Injuns lived here a long time 'fore white folks moved in. And these Injuns were special, not like any ol' Injun back then. Angels had given these Injuns the power to see things 'fore they happened. They knew they weren't gonna be 'round that much longer when the white folks rolled in. And the leaf readers believed…"

Larry Whitaker stopped mid-sentence when he saw the old, beaten-up white pickup drive by slowly. A grotesquely large man sat in the driver's seat. His shaved head gleamed in the sun, and he looked very pale, like some cave-dwelling creature that had never seen the light of day.

Larry Whitaker, Kate, and Kevin watched the truck go by. The large bald man glared into the Store at the three of them until the truck disappeared behind the tree line as the road twisted on in toward the heart of the Gorge.

Larry Whitaker shook his head and coughed. "You'ns better be gettin' on. It's about time for me to lie down for a bit," he said, rising from the stool and making his way from behind the counter.

"Could you tell us a little more about the White-Sight, leaf readers, and the Native Americans?" Kate asked with the tone of a teacher's pet.

"I've said too much already. You'ns gas on up and go, so I can lie down," Larry Whitaker said, nudging Kevin and Kate out the front door that he locked behind them.

Kevin turned around and watched frail, old fingers grab the open sign and flip it around.

Closed.

****

"Come on now, JJ," Larry Whitaker said, backing into the wall.

He'd cut the power off. Larry Whitaker knew JJ had come when he tried his bedside lamp, and it didn't come on. Larry knew he was in trouble the moment he saw JJ drive by when those university folks were asking all them questions about White-Sight and leaf reading.

Larry slid down the wall slowly, coming to a sitting position. JJ Conn loomed in the light of the moon, leaning forward and smiling down into Larry's face.

JJ's voice was quiet and calm. Larry wouldn't call it soothing. Not by any stretch of the imagination would you call it soothing. If you heard it without seeing *that* face you'd be tempted to think that, at first. Then something about the tone, you never could tell just what, would make the hair on the back of your neck stand on end. *Something's wrong*, the voice told you. *Something is wrong and you're not going to like the way I'm going to fix it.*

"I didn't tell 'em nothing. I told you what I told 'em. Please. For the love of God, JJ. Don't do this." Larry could not hide the panic in his voice. "Come on, now. You know me. I've been hearing you preach since

44

you was thirteen years old." He raised his hands to his face. "I helped ye bury Kade. I took the living water on your account."

JJ Conn leaned in closer, his nose nearly touching Larry's, covering his face in hot, fetid breath, the smile working its way up the pale cheeks.

"Oh, Lord. Jesus," Larry Whitaker said.

****

"I gotta go, darlin'," David Terry said.

Terry flipped the cell phone closed, walked over to his closet, and pulled on a pair of khakis. He turned back to the blonde looking up out of the mess of sheets and pillows.

"You gotta get on," Terry said. "I'm sorry. I gotta go back in."

Terry pulled the shirt he'd worn the day before over his head, most of the buttons still fastened, then the loosened tie which he'd tugged into place.

"Why do people gotta go and git kilt at three in the mornin'?" the blonde asked, standing up out of the bed, stark naked.

"You know the most of 'em don't really plan on it," he answered.

Terry pulled on his shoes and fumbled with the laces, watching the blonde walk across the room, then disappear into the bathroom. He finished tying, stood up, and grabbed his coat.

"Lock it up on your way out, would you please?" Terry called on his way out the front door.

He crossed the dew-covered yard and got into the cruiser.

The radio mumbled.

"Ten four. I'm en route," Detective David Terry

said.

****

"You said you was here yesterday?" Terry asked.

"Yessir, 'round 'bout noon. I came in to get a bite to eat," Henry Carthy said, shaking his head slowly. "I just caint figure why anyone'd do that for."

"Was anyone else in here when you found him this morning, Mr. Carthy?" Terry asked.

From the seat in the booth, Terry watched a deputy light a cigarette as he talked into his cell phone. The deputy walked over to one of the two gas pumps and leaned against it.

"No, sir. Just Larry back there in all that blood." Mr. Carthy kept shaking his head slowly, back and forth, back and forth.

"Excuse me for a second, Mr. Carthy," Terry said, sticking his head out the door.

"Mullens, get your ass away from the pump," Terry yelled.

He let the door swing shut and walked back to the cracked, yellow booth where Henry Carthy sat, shaking his head.

"Was he pretty well gone when you found him? Did he say anything to you?" Terry asked.

"No, sir. He didn't say nothing. He looked pretty well dead to me. Didn't see no breathing, but I damn sure didn't go over there and check for no pulse. On account of all that blood and all," Mr. Carthy said.

"Ok. Thank you kindly, Mr. Carthy. Why don't you get on home for some rest? I know this's been rough on you," Terry said, stepping out of the yellow booth.

"You'll catch whoever's done this, won't ye?" Mr.

Carthy asked.

"I'll do my damnedest, Mr. Carthy." Terry shook Henry Carthy's hand, then held the Store's front door open for him.

****

"I still can't wrap my head around how much of a bitch this would've been to build," Kevin said, sliding a little lower into the hot tub.

Kate nodded her assent.

"Think about hauling all the materials on this little gravel goat path, then across the creek and up that last steep part to the top of this ridge. Jesus, I'm glad I'm in science," Kevin said, shaking his head and smiling.

"I think getting in here every day is going to spoil us," Kate said, opening her eyes. "It's gonna be rough going back to downtown Lexington after this. We can do whatever we want to out here, and there's no one around to tell us otherwise."

Kate laughed and sat straight up in the hot tub. She slowly glided across to where Kevin was sitting with both of his arms propped on the sides. Kate, resting her knees on the seat, sat down on Kevin's lap, facing him.

"We can do whatever we want," Kate said in a low, throaty voice, just barely audible over the hot tub's jets. She gave Kevin her most seductive smile and reached one hand behind her back. Kate's bikini top splashed down into the hot tub and immediately disappeared into the maelstrom.

****

"White-Sight and Injuns and Bertie Mae and Elvis. Come on down from the mountain, Lauralee. We got work to do." Kevin's voice twanged out the words.

Kate rolled forward, grabbing her stomach over the

top of the seatbelt, not able to control the laughter.

Kevin mimicked Larry Whitaker's high, nasally cackle and continued, "Now, don't you lose it now. You'ns got dishes to warsh and floors ta sweep. Git on up to the house 'fore I bus' you one," Kevin said and laughed with Kate, nearly swerving into the guardrail.

"Jesus, Kevin," Kate said, still choking on her laughter.

"Shit. You'd think I's bin hitting that thar' mason jar of shine," Kevin said, wiping the smile from his face with pretend seriousness.

Kevin pulled around the curve and nearly came to a stop. The Store's small parking lot was filled with police cars, an ambulance, and a small fire truck. An older man in a fedora walked past the pumps to a small pickup truck, slowly shaking his head.

"Should we pull in and see what's going on?" Kate asked.

The old man's mouth was moving like he was saying something to himself.

"I don't know. We might get in their way. It's not really any business of ours anyway," Kevin said, easing the car forward.

They drove by the Store slowly, both of their necks craned out the passenger side window. A stout man in a tie and khakis watched them from just behind the front door.

The sharp bellow of the old truck's horn brought Kevin's attention back to the road. He cut the sport utility vehicle back into his lane and slammed on the brakes. They came to a complete stop, and for a long moment, Kevin stared into the eyes of a ghastly, tall man. There was a smile on his face, but it did not appear to be of the comforting variety in the slightest.

The man lifted his left hand from the steering wheel and stuck his elongated pointer finger out the open window at them. He shook it once, twice, then pulled away slowly, never taking his eyes from Kevin's.

Kevin and Kate looked at each other in silence, their mouths hanging open.

"What the hell was that?" Kate asked.

"I think we better take the long way back to the Red Tin. I don't want that cretin anywhere near me," Kevin said, pushing the gas pedal down.

****

Kate unzipped her backpack and dug around in the outermost pocket until she found the small leather-bound notebook. She flipped to a page labeled "occurrences" and followed the small table down to the last line where she wrote "new occurrence." Kate bent back to the pack and fished out the GPS. She wrote their coordinates into the book and slid the book into a pocket on the inside of her jacket and dropped the GPS back into the pack.

"I didn't expect to find any dago albo over here. We must've trampled over forty years' worth of old campfires and a couple of fresh ones, too," Kevin said.

Kate smiled at the excitement in his voice.

Kevin dropped to his knees, sweeping his hands around the small, young plants.

"It's just like Christmas, ain't it?" Kate asked, leaning her pack against the rockhouse wall.

Kevin turned his head toward Kate and, for a second, seemed embarrassed but grinned anyway.

"It's just neat, you know? Doesn't take much to

upset the habitat of these little guys. They grow on shallow, sandy soil on top of sandstone. A two-year-old could stomp across this patch and completely wipe 'em out," Kevin said.

Kate saw the invisible toddler make his way over the plants like a little Godzilla. She slid the water bottle out of the side pocket of the pack and took a swig. She held the bottle down to Kevin and looked out over the valley. It had taken them a few hours to get to this spot, weaving their way along the old hunting trails and animal paths. The park didn't have an official trail to this occurrence. The upkeep would have to be constant, which would be too costly for the ever-dwindling park budget. There were paths that weaved around the lower part of the ridge, including several stops along the river with deep, cool swimming holes. They started on one of these but damn near had to blaze their own path for the last two hours of the hike.

Kevin took the bottle and swallowed a drink. Kate watched him as he kept his eyes on the plants like he thought they'd disappear if he turned away.

"Hey, why don't you let me tally 'em up while you do a quick onceover for any more environmental damage, aside from the fires?" Kevin said, handing the bottle back.

Kate unzipped her jacket and pulled out the notebook and pen and gave them to Kevin. She retrieved the camera from the bag and put the strap around her neck, then zipped the jacket back up.

"You are happy to see this group," Kate said.

"Just don't stray too far. We only need about twenty yards or so for the write up," Kevin said, flipping through the notebook.

Kate walked around Kevin on the narrow overhang underneath the towering rock shelter ceiling. She moved across the ledge and around the rock into the forest. The shelter of the rockhouse had shielded the wind. Now it whipped her face, and she couldn't stop her eyes from watering. She pulled the hoodie from beneath her jacket and covered her head with it.

The ridge was surprisingly quiet; all Kate could hear was the constant whine of the wind. The trees around and below her swirled and danced, and she thought she could almost hear the sound of the branches groan while brushing together.

Kate walked up the steep bank and climbed atop the rockhouse. She watched a lone car weave in and out of vision on what Kate guessed was Red's Hollow Road but very well could've been the yellow brick road for all she knew. They'd covered, at least, six miles already. Six miles of unmarked trail used primarily by hunters and animals. Her feet ached in her shoes, but she couldn't help but feel happy. Nature always made her that way. As she often did, she turned over the words, wonderfully worn into her mind, that had changed her life forever so long ago. They came from the late Carl Sagan's reflections on a photograph of Earth taken by Voyager 1:

"Consider again that dot. That's here. That's home. That's us. On it everyone you love, everyone you know, everyone you ever heard of, every human being who ever was, lived out their lives. The aggregate of our joy and suffering, thousands of confident religions, ideologies, and economic doctrines, every hunter and forager, every hero and coward, every creator and destroyer of civilization, every king and peasant, every young couple in love, every mother and father, hopeful child, inventor and explorer, every teacher of morals, every corrupt politician, every 'superstar,' every 'supreme leader,' every saint and sinner in the history of our species lived there—on a mote of dust suspended in a sunbeam."

Kate watched the clouds roll over the valley as she climbed up and imagined how fractional she was. A speck of a speck on that "mote of dust." The river should've seemed so far down from her vantage point there, high up on the ridge, but in her reverie, it didn't seem so great a distance.

The world was such a beautiful place, and Kate felt so lucky to be alive, to be able to love and work. To laugh, cry, kiss, eat, and fuck. It was all so wonderful. Kate wiped a tear from her cheek and laughed out loud.

God, I can be so damn corny sometimes.

She came across a few empty beer cans and cigarette butts of which she took pictures. Kate walked past the patchy grass and soil out onto the sandstone bluff of the rockhouse. She bent down, then dropped to her stomach. She crawled on her belly, careful not to scratch the camera, out on the ledge until she looked down over the valley. She snapped several photos, then set the camera aside and enjoyed the view.

****

They'd just showered and were sitting down to rest for a while when there was a knock at the Red Tin's door. Kevin and Kate shared an uncertain glance. Then Kevin stood up and walked across the living room. He stood in front of the door but didn't open it right away.

"Who is it?" Kevin called.

"Detective David Terry of the Kentucky State

Police," the voice said.

Kevin opened the door.

"Can I help you?" Kevin asked.

"I sure hope so, mister…" Det. Terry said, waiting for Kevin to offer his name.

For a second, the two men stood there, watching each other in silence.

"Ballard. Dr. Kevin Ballard," Kevin said. He then asked Det. Terry in and pulled a chair out from underneath the kitchen table for him to sit in.

"Thank you, Dr. Ballard," Det. Terry said, shutting the door and settling into the seat.

Kate crossed the living room and stood in the doorway.

Det. Terry smiled and nodded his head in her direction.

"Afternoon, ma'am," he said.

"This is Katherine Johnson, Det. Terry," Kevin said.

Kate joined the two men at the table.

"What's going on?" she asked.

Det. Terry looked from Katherine Johnson to Dr. Kevin Ballard and smiled.

"I was hoping you all could tell me," he said. "I saw you all drive by Larry Whitaker's store this morning. You all drove by real slow, getting a good, long look. Then you damn near ran into JJ Conn. I heard that bastard's crazy and liable to kill you for something like that."

Kevin turned to Kate. He remembered the man in the white truck that pointed at them, but it had felt like he'd done so much more than just point. They both felt dirty, tainted afterward and went on back to the Red Tin and soaked in the hot tub for nearly two hours. Kevin thought he saw fear or something similar register on Kate's face.

"Yes, sir, we drove by the Store this morning," Kevin said, turning back to Det. Terry.

"Do you all know Larry Whitaker?" Det. Terry asked.

"No, sir. Well, not really. We talked to him yesterday for the first time," Kevin said.

Det. Terry reached into his breast pocket and pulled out a small notepad and pen. He flipped the pad open and clicked the button of the stainless steel retractable pen. "What were you all doing at the Store yesterday?" he asked, looking up from the notepad at Kevin, then Kate.

"We pulled in there to get some gas," Kevin said.

"'Round about what time would you say you all 'pulled in there to get some gas'?" Det. Terry asked.

Kevin looked over at Kate.

"It was after we got back from White's Branch Arch," Kevin said.

"I'd say around three, three-thirty," Kate said.

Kevin nodded and said, "Sounds about right."

Det. Terry scribbled briefly into his notepad, shut it, and set it on the table. He clicked the pen's button on the cover of the notepad like it'd flatlined and he was doing chest compressions waiting for the doctor to arrive.

Click, click, click, rocking the table slightly.

"What did you all and Mr. Whitaker talk about yesterday afternoon?" Det. Terry asked, keeping a steady rhythm with the pen.

Kate gasped. Kevin and Det. Terry looked over at

her. Kate's face was white, and she covered her mouth with her hands.

"Kate, what's wrong?" Kevin reached across the table and put his hand on her forearm.

"Something happened to him. Something bad, didn't it?" Kate asked Det. Terry through her trembling hands.

Det. Terry watched her, his eyes narrowing. Kevin looked from Kate to the detective.

"Yes, ma'am. Something bad did indeed happen to Larry Whitaker," he said, the pen still clicking steadily. "What do you know about this bad thing that happened to him?"

"Now hold on one sec—" Kevin started.

"He said he told us too much. He said that. Oh, God. Don't you remember, Kevin?" Kate said, her hands shooting down from her mouth and crashing onto the table in fists.

Det. Terry stopped clicking his pen. "What did Larry Whitaker tell you all too much about?" he asked.

Chapter Five

What Kevin Ballard found behind the closed bedroom door, the one he used to sleep behind and in which he spent most of his formative years behind, was a neat, clean room with a single tealight candle burning on the windowsill. The wax had melted out of its small aluminum holder and formed a hardened pile on the carpet. His mother had washed and changed the bedding in preparation of his visit; he could smell the clean linen. She hadn't kept his room the same as some parents did. The furniture and curtains had been updated, the walls repainted. There was a new light fixture.

Kevin stepped into the room and felt surprisingly let down. He'd geared himself up for this confrontation with the monster that had butchered his mother. He checked under the bed and inside the closet, knowing he wouldn't find anyone. Kevin opened the curtains and looked out the window into the darkness.

What a mess, he thought. He wanted to be anywhere else, under any other circumstances.

Kevin turned from the window and headed for the door, but something caught his eye on the bed. A copy of his book, *Nolin & the Hellbenders*, leaned against the pillows, the book cover facing out toward the foot of the bed. Kevin walked over to the bed and sat down. He stared at the book for a moment, as if he expected it to do something. Kevin grabbed it and looked it over. There was nothing out of the ordinary about the front cover, back cover, the top, side, or bottom of the pages, nothing on the spine.

Kevin had sent his mother a copy of *Nolin & the Hellbenders* just after it was published. He wrote his mother a note on the title page. Kevin assumed this was the copy he'd sent and turned to the title page for verification. The pages were stuck. He pried them apart carefully, without any ripping or tearing. There was his signature and message for his mother, but it was covered in dark red blood. The same message from the wall downstairs: *Repent, Sinner*.

"Oh, God," Kevin said, letting the book drop to the floor.

****

The police arrived not ten minutes later. Kevin was sitting on the front porch with the bottle of bourbon and a can of cola. He wasn't drunk, but he felt he damn sure couldn't be sober any longer. He took sips from the bottle and chased it with the soda while the sheriff's deputy asked him questions. Kevin answered all of them.

Then another sheriff's deputy arrived. Then an ambulance that was followed by the sheriff-elect himself and then two boys from the state police, a trooper, and a detective. Kevin sat on the porch in the worn rocking chair while the police went about their business. He answered any additional questions anyone asked, but other than that, he sat there quietly with the bourbon and cola.

When they had conducted what needed conducting, the EMT brought out his mother's body in a black bag on top of a gurney. They took her across the porch, up the walk, then lifted her into the ambulance.

Kevin left his drinks on the table on the front porch and went back in the house. He made a pot of coffee and sat on the counter, his back to the dining room table, and waited for the coffee to finish brewing. He'd heard footsteps upstairs, so he was not surprised when one of the deputies entered the kitchen a few moments later.

"Dr. Ballard, I'm awful sorry about what happened to your mother," the deputy said.

Kevin looked up from the counter at the deputy and thanked him for the condolences. He plopped down from the counter and walked over to the coffee pot. He pulled a coffee mug from the cabinet and hesitated before closing the cabinet. The deputy still stood there in the kitchen watching him.

"Would you like a cup of coffee?" Kevin asked.

The deputy adjusted his pants in the front and appeared to be considering the offer.

"No, I better not," he said. "Gotta get back to the office and get the paperwork started. I'm awful sorry about your mother."

Kevin nodded his head twice and shut the cabinet. He poured himself a cup and got the creamer from the refrigerator and poured a dollop in and stirred.

The deputy still stood there.

"Dr. Ballard. Your momma, she went to church with me and my family. She talked about you an awful lot. She said she was afraid for your soul." The deputy looked uncomfortable with the topic he was pressing, but press it he did.

Kevin felt resentment rise up but stomached it

down with a sip of the hot coffee.

"Did she?" he asked.

The deputy nodded. "Your momma said she and your daddy knew you were smart. They said you were much smarter than they had ever even hoped to be themselves. Your momma said she just couldn't understand why you would use all that intelligence on something so trivial as genes and cells and plants and animals. She said she used to dream that you'd grow up and lead a new generation of religious philosophy," he said.

Kevin looked up from the coffee at the deputy. A little gold bar on his chest read: Deputy S. Ferguson.

"Deputy Ferguson, are you intending on standing in my dead mother's kitchen and lecturing me on my professional career and personal beliefs?" Kevin couldn't contain the edge in his voice. "Because if you do so intend to take this course of action, I might be inclined to throw your ass out by the seat of those *awful* tight little pants of yours."

Deputy Ferguson looked like he'd been slapped. His mouth hung open. Then he began to stammer like a relay firing off but not finding any connective synapses.

Kevin slammed the cup on the counter, chipping the bottom and sloshing the contents. He glared at the deputy and felt like leaping across the kitchen and smashing it in that stunned, stupid face.

The deputy regained his composure and said, "Well, I can see that your momma's concerns were warranted. I hope you can see what a mess you've made by the things you've chosen to believe. The world is a dangerous place, and I think your chickens have come home to roost."

****

After the police had cleared out, Kevin was left alone in his parents' house. They had built the house just after they'd had him. One of Kevin's earliest memories was of his father and mother down on their hands and knees, ripping the carpet up. They'd decided they'd rather have hardwood floors after three years of living with carpet.

Kevin looked down at the floor and realized he still had his shoes on. His mother would have pitched a fit. Three years of living with a house completely carpeted had given her a new pet peeve—shoes. She made everyone leave their shoes at the door. She swept the floors daily and mopped three times a week during the middle of the day, just in time to watch *General Hospital*.

Now she was gone.

Kevin still didn't fully believe that his father was gone, and he had died nearly ten years ago. His mother had died only a few hours ago, and it felt realer than anything Kevin had ever held to be real. All that blood.

Kevin walked down the hall to the small closet under the stairs where his mother kept the broom and mop and other cleaning supplies. He grabbed a bucket, dumped a heavy helping of bleach into it, then went into his mother's bathroom, and set it under her bathtub faucet. He wrenched the handle as far to the left as it would go and filled the bucket with nearly scorching water.

His mother's soap, the same she'd used since he was kid, filled his nostrils, and tears brimmed in his eyes.

Kevin took the steaming bucket down the hall, into

the kitchen, where he pulled out the dish soap from under the sink, where she'd always kept it, and squeezed a heavy stream in with the water and the bleach. He set the bucket on the counter nearest the kitchen table and walked back down the hall to get the scouring pads and cleaning rags.

****

The first of the day's sun streaked in the deck door windows and reflected off the shining table and floor. Kevin had just poured himself the last cup of coffee from the third pot he'd had since arriving at his parents' house the night before. He'd spent the night on his hands and knees, scrubbing away his mother's blood from the hardwood kitchen floor he'd watched her and his father lay.

He'd started with the dining room table, then moved to the floor around it. Then he swept and mopped the entirety of the hardwood flooring from his mother's bedroom, down the hall into the mudroom, and on into the kitchen and dining room. The living room was the only room on the first floor that was carpeted.

He had to empty and change the water in the bucket out continuously. The bucket was blue and gave the bloody water a purple hue that was nearly black. He had taken off his collared shirt early on in the cleaning, and now his forearms up to the elbow were tainted red. The house smelt of a mixture of bleach and copper.

Kevin took pictures of everything before he cleaned. He didn't consciously do so but noticed about three pictures in that he was documenting the house as if it were a case study. His mind was already turning over sentences like, "The vast majority of the blood was spilled onto the dining room table with a large amount of runoff spilling onto the surrounding floor."

He'd scrubbed the message off the living room wall last of all. He almost couldn't do it. He stood barefooted in the living room, his arms and feet stained, and stared at the wall. He read each of the words as if they were their own sentences and paragraphs. They took on pages of meanings of their own.

Repent.

Sinner.

Repent, sinner.

A mantra of confusion. *What? Why? How?*

With the first light of the day and after his last cup of coffee, Kevin walked down the hall to his parents' bedroom and slept.

****

Kevin's dreams twisted and turned, carrying him well past midafternoon. He dreamed of being young, being taken care of by both of his parents. He dreamed his mother was a child lying butchered on the dining room table. Kevin dreamed of a fire by the mountainside, then an explosion.

****

Kevin woke to the sound of his mother's name being called. He rose out of the depths of his dreams and sat up in his parents' bed.

"Mrs. Ballard? Evelyn Ballard?" the voice called out.

Kevin swung his legs off the side of the bed and sat, listening.

"Mrs. Ballard, are you there?"

Kevin rose to his feet and crossed the bedroom to the hall. He pictured his mother just getting up from the couch, where she sat with a steaming cup of freshly brewed coffee, waiting for him to wake up, and walking to answer the door.

Knocking.

"Mrs. Ballard?"

Kevin walked down the hallway. He didn't see anyone outside the front door. He turned to the living room. His mother was not sitting at the couch as he'd imagined her. A weight dropped into his stomach, and Kevin thought for a second he was going to be sick. His mother was dead. She had been killed in this very house only hours before, and there had been blood. Lots and lots of blood.

Kevin walked into the living room, shaking his head.

"Dr. Ballard?" a voice called from behind the screen door, leading out onto the deck.

Kevin looked up to see a young man peering into the house through cupped hands.

"Yes. Can I help you?"

"I'm Brian Thomas. I go to church with your mom. Can I come in?"

Brian Thomas did not wait for an answer but slid the screen door open and stepped into the dining room.

"What can I help you with, Mr. Thomas?"

"It was you that found Angela last night, wasn't it?" Brian asked, plopping into a chair at the kitchen table.

Kevin expected a squishing sound, but there wasn't one. He had cleaned the table and chairs as thoroughly as he'd ever cleaned anything in his life.

"What?" Kevin asked.

"You was the one that found Angela dead at the

Sonora BP last night, wasn't you?" Brian said. His face was very pale and dark bags hung loosely under his eyes. He couldn't have been more than twenty years old, far too young to look so tired.

"What?"

Then Kevin remembered. The young girl's doe-eyed face swam back to him, and he saw all that blood again.

"Oh, God," Kevin said, shaking his head. "Yes. Yes, I was the one that found her. I didn't know her name. Did you know her?"

"Yes, I did. She was my girlfriend," Brian Thomas said. His voice sounded raw and husky. Tears filled his eyes.

"I'm sorry," Kevin said after a moment.

"What happened to her?" Brian asked.

Kevin looked away. He turned around toward the wall. It shined in the sunlight, freshly scrubbed.

"I'm not sure, Brian," Kevin said. "Something terrible."

Brian broke down. His head fell into his arms on the clean table and he sobbed.

Kevin turned back around and walked over to him. He patted his back and told him he was sorry. Kevin scrutinized the table, looking for any spots he might have missed. He didn't see any.

"All I know is that she was killed. I went there for gas last night on my way here, and I found her behind the counter," Kevin said, taking a step back and scanning the floor underneath and around the table.

Brian Thomas lifted his head from his arms and wiped the tears and snot on his shirt sleeve.

"Who did this?"

"I don't know," Kevin said, looking up from the floor to Brian.

"Was she alive when you saw her?"

"No. She was already gone."

"How…how did she die?" Brian asked.

"Somebody cut her, Brian. They cut her arms. She bled out," Kevin said.

Brian convulsed into sobs again and buried his face back into his arms on the table.

Shouldn't I be uncontrollable like this kid? Kevin thought. He knew the thought was ludicrous as soon as he'd had it. Each person reacted to tragedy in their own ways.

Kevin made another pot of coffee and sat on the counter, facing the table, alternately watching Brian Thomas cry and scanning the room for any blood he might've missed.

****

Brian said he'd found out about Angela's murder the previous night, after a friend of his at the sheriff's office called and told him. Brian said his friend had also told him that Evelyn Ballard's son was the one who'd found her and called 911. Brian said he looked up Evelyn Ballard's phone number in the church directory and tried calling all last night.

Brian was up and pacing the length of the dining room, into the kitchen and back. Kevin still sat on the counter with a cup of coffee. He had made one for Brian as well, but he hadn't touched it.

"I couldn't sleep at all last night," Brian said. "I couldn't sit down for longer than a few minutes. I just caint stop picturing her, man. Smiling and happy. I caint picture Angela dead. I just caint."

Brian Thomas hadn't mentioned Evelyn in the past tense once.

He doesn't know.

"You said you went to church with my mom. When was the last time you saw her?" Kevin asked.

Brian stopped pacing and looked over the dining room table at Kevin on the counter.

"I guess last Wednesday night. Why? Where is she?" Brian Thomas asked.

"Last Wednesday night," Kevin said. "At Severance Valley?"

"Yeah. Is she ok?"

"No. No, she's not. Did she seem worried or scared or anything like that when you saw her Wednesday night?" Kevin asked, setting the coffee mug down and jumping off the counter.

Brian's eyes widened, and he took a few steps closer to Kevin.

"No. She seemed ok. She didn't seem any different to me," he said.

Kevin Ballard stood at the head of the dining room table, looking hard at Brian Thomas. Kevin then leaned forward and placed both of his hands, palm down, onto the table.

"I found *her* last night as well. She was laying on this table with both of her wrists tore open. Just like Angela," Kevin said. He slid his palms across the table slowly and in small, caressing circles, the way some folks treat a tombstone.

"Oh, God," Brian Thomas said. He took a quick step away from the table, like it had suddenly burst into flames or the gruesome and ravaged body of Evelyn Ballard had suddenly appeared. He stared at the table for a moment before turning both of his forearms around and looking for any blood or bodily fluids. Kevin almost swore he could see Brian Thomas's brain working.

"Jesus, man. What happened?" Brian asked, bringing his attention back to Kevin.

"After I found Angela at the gas station, I drove on home, here," Kevin motioned from the deck doors to the kitchen with his right hand, "to find my mother butchered on the table and the power cut." Kevin paused to take a sip of the coffee, then continued, "She was laying right here. There were candles lit all over the house. There was blood on everything."

Kevin turned from the table to the living room and the wall that bore the message. He pointed at it with the coffee mug. "And on that wall right there, the bastard left a message. He took his bare hands and covered them in my mother's blood, then wrote on the wall. He wrote it with his goddamn fingers like a kindergartener. 'Repent, Sinner.'"

Kevin Ballard and Brian Thomas both stared at the wall as if the message hadn't been washed off, as if it were right there in front of them in all its sanguine atrocity.

Kevin watched Brian Thomas as he soundlessly mouthed the words to himself. *Repent, Sinner.*

Brian turned slowly to Kevin.

"You work for UK, don't you?" Brian said. It wasn't really a question. "You published that book on evolution and lizards or whatever."

Kevin narrowed his eyes on Brian. He saw the bloody title page of *Nolin & the Hellbenders*.

"Yes?" Kevin said.

"You don't think this could've been on account of you writing that?" Brian asked.

Kevin's head rolled back on his neck, like he'd just been hit in the teeth with a brick.

"Are you saying that somebody killed my mother because I got my doctoral thesis published?" Kevin hadn't realized he had raised his voice until he heard it bounce off the living room walls.

The two men stood there in silence for some time, not looking at each other. In the backyard, the Nolin River murmured on toward the lake, and the sun snuck behind a sterling white cumulus cloud.

Chapter Six

When she awoke, Kate found that both her hands and feet were bound together. A bandana was tied around her head, covering her mouth. Something sour-tasting and cottony was in her mouth. Her head felt like a balloon, pushed to the point of explosion, now limp with full-deflation.

A small window covered by a tattered confederate flag glowed with a yellow tint. It was daytime. How long had she been out? She had just settled into a hot bath when she heard someone. Someone had been in the bathroom of the Red Tin. It hadn't been any voice she recognized. Kate shuddered despite the hot, stale air bearing down on her.

It looked like a singlewide trailer. She was sitting on stained carpet, leaned against a wood paneled wall straight across from the confederate-flagged window. To her right, she saw a small bar and walkway into what appeared to be the kitchen; she could just barely see the silver glint of the sink. To her left, she saw the front door and a hallway that she assumed led to the bedrooms. There wasn't a thing in the room other than herself and the stained flag.

Kate tried to climb to her feet but lost her balance and plopped back down on the dirty carpet. She realized she was nearly naked. She had on only a very large, worn T-shirt. She felt the itchy carpet brush against her uncovered bottom.

She shuddered in revulsion. Who knows what kind of filth was on this carpet. Her mind then shot back to the bathtub. She had been completely naked then. Someone had covered her with this shirt, which wasn't her shirt. Someone had handled her, dressed her, taken her.

Kate's stomach sank. She gagged at the awful taste in her mouth. She tried to stop herself, but she vomited and, with tearing eyes, had to half-swallow, half-chew it back down around the filthy sock or whatever it was that was in her mouth.

****

"All I'm saying is that what you say doesn't just affect you," Brian Thomas said.

"So I'm not supposed to publish any scientific findings that don't correlate with what you believe down there at Severance Valley?" Kevin said, the last bit in an exaggerated drawl.

Brian's face reddened, his hands clenched into fists. "Your mother talked about you. She said she was scared of the things you believed and the things you *didn't* believe. She said she wanted you to go to Heaven, but she was afraid you wouldn't because you didn't believe in God. She also said she was scared somebody might hurt you for the things you said or wrote."

Kevin thought Brian Thomas looked like one of those people at that moment.

"You people are nuts." Kevin dismissed Brian Thomas with a wave of his hand. "You all want to control every aspect of everybody's lives. You got your grubby, little meddling fingers into everything. Well past your goddamn boundaries. Extended long past your capacity for understanding." His laugh was sharp, condemning.

"Look at you. All smart, high, and mighty. Got yourself a D and a R in front of your name, but where has it gotten you? It got your mother killed. That's where it got you, *Doctor* Ballard," Brian Thomas said and stormed past Kevin, bumping into his shoulder.

Kevin didn't follow him and didn't worry about any attack from behind. He heard the loud steps, the front door open, then slam shut, rattling the trinkets in the windowsills.

****

Kevin remembered being young and going to church with his parents. His mother was always a cheerful person, but on Sunday mornings, she positively radiated warmth. She woke before James and Kevin and ironed their clothes, along with her own. After, she hung the clothes in the hall closet, and she made breakfast. She'd fry bacon, then eggs. She'd make a pot of oatmeal, then silver dollar pancakes.

Kevin still associated the wonderful scent of frying bacon with Sunday mornings and his mother. It's what woke him up, brought him out of the warm blankets, into the sun-filled kitchen where he'd slide into a chair at the table or atop a stool at the bar.

His mother would stop whatever she was doing when she saw Kevin, and for one beautiful moment, she would just smile at him. Then she'd say breakfast would be ready in a jiffy and get back to it.

Kevin sat atop a stool at the bar, looking out the kitchen window at the front yard and the county road beyond it. A bowl of cold, soggy cereal half-eaten was in front of him and, next to it, his cell on speakerphone, calling Kate. It rang and rang. Then the voicemail clicked on.

"Hello. You've reached Kate Johnson. I'm sorry I'm not able to—" Kate said through the recorded message.

Kevin ended the call and hit redial. Again, the call went unanswered.

A heavy weight had settled on Kevin's chest. Why wasn't Kate answering? It was nearly noon. She'd definitely be awake by now, probably had been for hours. Kevin shifted uneasily on the stool, then took another bite of the Great Grains. He chewed, not really tasting anything but the milk—whole milk, his mother always kept whole milk in the house.

****

In the Sunday paper, on the front page toward the bottom, was a short piece about the death of a troubled area teen. According to the article, Angela Rogers took her own life that Friday. Inquiries had been made to the police and coroner's office, who both issued statements that more information would follow, but all initial reports indicated suicide.

****

"Let us turn to the Book of Isaiah together," the congenial, deep southern voice said through the PA system.

A vast shuffling sounded through the open church.

Kevin snorted quietly to himself at the thought of the word *church* being used to described Severance Valley; it looked more like a converted factory.

"Now let us read chapter forty, verse eight," the voice said.

A few hundred voices reading softly together. A chorus of ethereal murmurs whispering in tandem: "The grass withers, the flower fades, but the word of our God will stand forever."

The communal voice dissipated slowly as several stragglers finally finished.

"Amen," the congregation repeated after the loud speaker.

Kevin looked up from his interlocked hands to those around him. They'd all bowed their heads, reading, whispering. Now they turned their eyes expectantly to the pulpit, the raised stage at the front of the cavernous room. The lights dimmed above the pews, and a faint trumpet moaned out through the speakers. An expanse of lighting above the stage flashed on with several bright colors, then dimmed to just one white spotlight shining directly above the pastor, Dr. David Cessaurs.

Kevin wanted to scream. He wanted to chuck the Bible and hymnal at Dr. David Cessaurs and scream at each and every one of the brain-dead sheep that glared at him out the corner of their eyes after telling him how sorry they were for his loss. His *loss*, each and every one of them emphasized the word, but their eyes said more. He was the cause of his loss, the eyes said. If he hadn't said those blasphemous words, Evelyn Ballard would still be sitting in this multimillion-dollar warehouse chanting to the great emptiness they swore was filled with an all-powerful, all-knowing yet personal prayer-answering, invisible friend.

Dr. David Cessaurs thanked them for coming and said, "Our Evelyn would have appreciated your presence here in a place she held so dearly."

73

Doctor? Right, Kevin thought. He'd had to bust his ass for years after carefully choosing a topic worthy of research. He'd designed, redesigned, and conducted experiments and read book after book of material, not to mention hour upon hour of field work. In the end, he had completed and submitted and defended his thesis and earned his doctorate.

Dr. David Cessaurs had read the Bible. He'd read the Bible and a few religious books by a few well-known preachers and probably taken an online quiz and was awarded his *doctorate*, if it could ever really measure up to be such. The word almost seemed cheapened by the man's attainment of it.

"Evelyn Ballard had been a member of this church long before we built this sanctuary and grew into the family we are now. Evelyn was with us when we were in a little brick building with three pews and a row of foldout chairs. She's worked in the nursery and has taught Sunday school. Watched your children, taught them the powerful stories of the Bible and all with a kind, gentle heart." Dr. Cessaurs smiled and looked out at the congregation.

Kevin sat scowling in the front row next to his aunt, Bonnie Williams, his mother's sister. She'd shown up at the house not an hour after Brian Thomas had stormed out. He was still sitting on the stool when she came through the door. He jumped at the opening of the door but smiled when he saw her.

"I didn't hear you pull up," Kevin said, walking across the kitchen and hugging her.

"Oh, Kevin. I'm so sorry," Aunt Bonnie said, pulling him close and squeezing surprisingly hard for a woman in her mid-sixties.

"What in God's name happened down here?" she asked, pulling away but holding Kevin's triceps, keeping him close on account of her nearsightedness. Aunt Bonnie's eyes were huge and blurry through her thick glasses.

Kevin did not know how to answer her. He opened and shut his mouth several times before just shaking his head slowly from right to left and back again.

"Only God knows," she said sadly and pulled Kevin in for another hug. "But don't you worry 'bout a thing now. Aunt Bonnie's here and will handle all of this. You hear?"

Sitting next to Aunt Bonnie on the pew in the grotto of the megachurch, Kevin was thankful that his aunt had come. She'd swooped in, taken him under her wing, and helped him handle all of the things associated with the death of a loved one. She'd talked to the insurance company, the Social Security Administration, the funeral home, the church, and the family and friends. Kevin reached over and took his aunt's hand. She looked over at him, and Kevin saw that she'd been crying.

****

Kevin tried her cell again but didn't get an answer. He opened his contacts on the phone, scrolled down until he found Biology Department and called. Kinders answered.

"Ballard, how's it going over there in the sticks'n'hills?"

"Not good, Kinders. Have you seen or heard from Kate?"

Kinders laughed that asshole laugh of his, high and nasally. "Uh-oh. Has Bahward wost his whittle gurfrwen?" Kinders' attempt at a small child's voice. It was apparent Kinders hadn't spent much time around children, which Ballard thought was in their best interest anyway, or had been in contact with only Asian immigrant children.

"Kinders, I'm serious. I'm back in Hardin County right now, and I haven't heard from her since I left," Kevin said.

"I don't know what you think the Biology Department is, but it for sure isn't your own personal dating service and concierge. The department isn't responsible for keeping tabs on your girlfriend. Why don't you drive back to your little love bungalow and check on her? Afraid she might be knocking boots with one of the locals?"

"I'm not in the mood for your bullshit right now, Kinders. I'm in Hardin County because my mother died. She was fucking killed. You know, *murdered*. So I'd appreciate a little goddamn courtesy." Kevin paused and took a large, shaky breath to calm himself.

"Now, I'm scared Kate might be in some sort of trouble. I think my mother was killed by some religious whackjob who's mistaken my book as sacrilegious or blasphemous or whatever," Kevin said. "Now, are you going to help me or not?"

For once, Kinders was rendered speechless. After a long, tense silence, he surprised Kevin again by offering to help. Ballard then proceeded to tell Kinders everything that had happened since he'd left to spend the weekend with his mother, from finding the body of Angela Rogers to the assistance of Aunt Bonnie.

"Let me try her from this phone. Maybe she's pissed at you or something. She might answer if she sees it's the department calling," Kinders said and hung up.

A few moments later, Kinders called back. They didn't bother with greetings.

"Nothing," he said.

"Shit," Kevin said. "Ok. I'm going to go talk to Aunt Bonnie and see that she wraps up everything here. I'll call the state police post in Morehead when I get on the road. I should be there in three hours, if I can get on the road in the next few minutes."

"Ok. I'll go check your apartment, then hers. I'll see if anybody in the department has seen her around or heard from her. Text me the address of the Red Gutter or whatever-the-fuck you said it was called, and I'll head that way afterward."

They were just getting ready to get off the phone, but Kevin stopped Kinders from hanging up.

"Kinders," Kevin said, "thank you. I really appreciate your help. I owe you big time."

"Don't worry about it, Ballard. I'm sorry for giving you such a hard time. I hope Kate's all right. Be careful. If you think this person killed your mom and may have hurt Kate, that paints a gigantic fucking bull's-eye on your chest. See you soon," Kinders said and ended the call.

****

Kevin met Aunt Bonnie back at his parents' home. There was another car parked in the driveway. Kevin groaned, thinking it was another distant relative or friend of the family come to relay their condolences. He opened the door and found his aunt sitting on the couch in the living room with an older man in a gray suit. They both set their mugs on the coffee table and stood.

"Kevin, this is your mother's attorney, Emmanuel Stephens. He's here to talk to you about your mother's will," Aunt Bonnie said, nodding to the man in the gray suit.

Emmanuel Stephens smiled the smile of those expressing their condolences, not too far away from a frown but enough of a smile to express goodwill. Emmanuel Stephens extended his hand to Kevin and said, "I'm sorry to hear about your mother, Mr. Ballard. I've known her for quite a few years now. Knew, I reckon is the term now." Emmanuel Stephens shook his head slowly and looked off toward the windows.

"I made a fresh pot of coffee, if you want some," Aunt Bonnie said.

"I actually need to speak with you in private, Aunt Bonnie," Kevin said. He turned to Emmanuel Stephens and said, "Is there any way this can wait until next week, Mr. Stephens?"

"Of course, of course," Mr. Stephens said. "I know how these things are, and I don't want to be any more of a burden on you than you've already got. So I'll just give you the highlight reel of it and get out of your hair. Your mother left you the house, land, boats, the whole kit and caboodle. She also left you some money and stocks, that sort of thing. She said her sister, your aunt Bonnie here, could have whatever furniture she wanted, clothes and things like that."

Kevin nodded his head quickly, thinking about Kate.

"Yes, sir. Ok. I'll call you next week and make an appointment," Kevin said.

"I'm only in the office on Thursdays now. See, I'm sort of retired," Mr. Stephens said.

"Fine. Thursday, it is. I'll see you then," Kevin said.

"Again, I'm sorry for your loss. Your mother was a good woman. I'll see you Thursday, Mr. Ballard," Mr. Stephens walked across the living room into the mudroom and slowly out the front door.

"Kevin, what's gotten into you? You were rude to that nice, old man."

"Aunt Bonnie, something's come up, and I've got to get on back. Would you please handle things here until I call you? Please?" Kevin tried to speak slowly, but he couldn't hide the panic in his voice.

"What's wrong, Kevin?" Aunt Bonnie asked, her face wrinkling.

"I'm afraid that whoever did this to Mom has done something to Kate, my girlfriend. I have to get back and try to find her."

Kevin walked down the hall to his parents' bedroom, his mother's, *his* bedroom now. He grabbed the duffle bag he'd left on the desk chair. He hadn't even really unpacked.

"Kevin, have you called the police about this? Don't you think that's what you need to do, instead of going out and trying to find her on your own?" Aunt Bonnie asked. She followed him through the house while he threw the few things he did unpack back into the duffle bag.

"I'm going to call them on my way out there. I've already called a..." Kevin paused, holding his toothbrush and toothpaste just above the bag. "...a friend from the university who is going to meet me at the cabin where Kate's supposed to be."

Kevin nodded at the word "friend," confirming it to

himself for the first time.

"Kevin. You hold on a minute here. Your mother isn't hours in the grave, and you're already going to fly out of here, scared and panicked? I think you need to sit down and just stay put. Call the police. Let them handle it. It's their job. They get paid to wear badges and tote guns. What you need to do is sit down on that couch out there and mourn the loss of your mother." Aunt Bonnie had placed both of her hands on Kevin's arms and leaned in close. Kevin stared into the fishbowl glasses at the moist eyes of his aunt. "Your mother is not coming back and nothing you do will change that. You don't need to get no high and noble ideas about going out there and catching the person that's done this."

Kevin breathed deep. Standing in his parents' bedroom with the door to the laundry room open, Kevin could smell the fragrance of his mother's perfume, as well the fabric softener she used on all the bedding and clothes. For a second, Kevin just stood there, letting the snapshots of memories turn over like a small, plastic pinwheel. His mother was sitting there, waiting on him with a steaming cup of coffee. His mother was folding laundry on her bed where he stood and helped. His mother was pulling a quilt up to his chin and kissing him goodnight. Then, she was lying in a pool of her coagulating blood on the dining room table, both wrists open to the bone.

"Oh, God," Kevin said, dropping his head onto his aunt's shoulder, tears streaming from his eyes.

"That's it," Aunt Bonnie said, running her thin fingers through Kevin's uncombed hair. "That's it, baby. It's ok."

****

It took nearly twenty minutes for Kevin Ballard to regain control of himself. He cried like a baby, like he hadn't cried since he'd been one. He hadn't even cried like that when his father died. He'd shed tears, sure, manly things that dropped from his eyes, despite his stonewalled face, but with his father's death came a more subtle hurt. He saw his father in the small things of everyday use. The bite marks on a pen when he took one out to write a thank you card. The dent in the front door frame where his father kicked the mud off his boots before taking them off and entering the house.

Now with his mother's death, it all came back full circle. Kevin was back in his parents' house, now *his* house, now that they were both gone, carefully tucked into a neatly manicured lawn under an old magnolia just outside of Elizabethtown, the city in which they were both born and in which they met and fell in love.

Kevin leaned against his mother's sister, his aunt, until the tears subsided and left him wet-faced and red-eyed. Then he disengaged himself from Aunt Bonnie and wiped his eyes and cheeks dry.

"Thank you," Kevin said.

She nodded, her own cheeks wet with tears.

"I needed that," he said. "Now I have to go."

Aunt Bonnie continued nodding, though not in approval, but in resigned acknowledgment.

****

Kevin Ballard phoned the state police post in Morehead as he barreled down the county road toward the highway. Late afternoon was bleeding on toward dusk, and he saw several pairs of eyes reflect in the headlights along the way.

He spoke with the operator, then dispatch. He'd

asked for Det. Terry, but he was not in the office. Kevin was placed on hold for several minutes before a brusque, deep voice came on the line.

"Mr. Ballard?" the voice said.

"Yes, sir. I'm here."

"This is Sergeant Polk. What's going on?"

Kevin relayed the events of his weekend to Sgt. Polk, who breathed steadily into the phone and listened until Kevin had finished talking.

"Where are you now?" Sgt. Polk asked.

"I'm almost to I-65," Kevin replied.

"And you're heading out to the Red Tin Cabin to see about your girlfriend, Katherine 'Kate' Johnson, the woman you fear might be in trouble?" Sgt. Polk said.

"Yes, sir. I've got a friend heading out there as well. He was gonna check our apartments in Lexington first," Kevin said, jerking the car into the center lane to avoid a possum.

"Who's the friend?" Sgt. Polk asked.

"Jason Kinders. He's a colleague from UK. I gave him the address and directions to the cabin. He should be there or on his way by now. I better call him," Kevin said.

"Mr. Ballard, tell him not to go to the cabin. Tell him to wait someplace and let a trooper check the place out. You need to do the same. Come on out this way if you feel you must, but don't go straight to the cabin. If what you're saying is true, the place could be dangerous," Sgt. Polk said.

Kevin opened his mouth to dissent when his phone vibrated against his cheek. He pulled the phone away from his ear and looked at the screen. A Lexington area phone number beeping in.

"Sgt. Polk, I'm getting another call. It might be Kinders. I'll call you right back," Kevin said, then hung up.

Kevin answered the call. "Hello?"

"Ballard. It's Kinders. I checked the apartments and didn't find her. I looked in through the windows and didn't see anything out of place. I'm on my way out to the cabin as we speak."

Kevin listened to the background noise and could tell Kinders was in a vehicle with the windows down.

"I'm on my way. I called KSP, and they said to wait before going to the cabin. They said it could be dangerous and they should be the ones to check it out," Kevin said.

Kinders snorted. "I'll do whatever you want me to, but I think the quicker we get to that cabin the better. If she's there and her phone just died or lost reception or whatever, and this person is targeting her next, then the sooner we get to her the better," Kinders said.

"I agree. I'm on my way. Call me as soon as you get there. Thank you, Kinders."

Kevin hung up the phone, then took the onramp and merged onto I-65. He called the state police again when he turned off I-65 onto the Bluegrass Parkway. He spoke with the operator and told her he'd been speaking with Sgt. Polk. He was put on hold. He waited on the line for several miles before hanging up and increasing his speed.

Chapter Seven

When she awoke again, it was dark. No shaded sun fell through the confederate flag-covered window. There were no lights on in the trailer. Kate moved up into a sitting position, her back against the wood paneling. She slowed her breathing down as much as possible and strained her ears, listening. Crickets. The faint hum of something mechanical. The even fainter hooting of an owl from somewhere behind the trailer.

Kate's eyes slowly adjusted to the darkness. She looked about the room and could see that it was still as empty as it had been. Then something caught her eye, something dark and nestled in the corner between the kitchen and the living room.

Kate peeled her eyes until they were narrow slits, trying to make out what lay under the darkness. Then it moved. It drew itself together, then towered nearly to the ceiling. It jerked itself forward and crossed the room until it stood before Kate, looming above her frightened face.

The shadow lengthened and sank down, level with Kate.

"While ye have light, believe in the light, that ye may be the children of the light. These things spake Jesus, and departed, and did hide himself from them," a quiet voice said in the night, and out of the darkness, Kate made out the face of a gigantic man.

****

Sgt. Polk had called Terry out of church. He'd been sitting there with Abigail and her mother, Francine, watching one of Abi's friends get dunked in the glass-partitioned whirlpool up front. Whatever chances Francine gave him to see Abigail, Terry snatched 'em up. He didn't care if it was going to church, PTA meetings, debate team conferences, just as long as he got to smile down on his little girl and wrap her up in his arms.

Terry used to feel the same about Francine, and he was sure, at some point, she must've felt that way about him, but they both knew those times were long passed. She got the house (and sold it) and what money there was in the divorce. He got every other weekend visitations with Abi—he got to see her more often than that, but every other weekend was the court-ordered minimum—and an empty, restful bed.

Terry was sitting there, next to Abi on the pew, looking out of the corner of his eye over Abi's blonde head at Francine while the pastor led the congregation in some mumbling prayer. He hadn't really been paying attention. He'd long held the belief that Francine was a faker. He watched her closed eyes and moving mouth for any sign of forgery or simulation. She had forced the issue of saying grace before supper and teaching Abigail to say her prayers on her knees at her bedside, but Terry couldn't help but always think it was just a ploy to look like the model mother. He didn't buy, for a second, that Francine Clark had found religion and turned over a new leaf, but she insisted Abi have some religion, too, and Terry didn't really think it mattered. Pray all you want, but what's going to happen is what's going to happen. Praying doesn't stop the bus.

Terry chuckled to himself there on the church pew as he remembered his first manslaughter case a few years before Abigail was born. He was fresh out of the academy, and they'd shipped him off to Post 9 in Pike County. He'd been on lunch over at the Dairy Cheer, stuffing his face with a Smashburger, when dispatch called him back in. An older gentleman had been crossing Hambley Boulevard in downtown Pikeville and was struck by a Medicare transportation shuttle bus.

By the time Terry got there, a large crowd surrounded the body. He made his way to the center, and there was the frail, old body of a man covered in blood and abrasions. A sweating, fat man stood, holding a Dale Jr. hat and shaking his head, tears falling from his eyes. He'd been the driver of the bus. Terry learned that the fat man knew the old man, had picked him up for several doctors' appointments at the medical center (he had black lung) as well as several visitations with his grandchildren, who were placed in foster care due to their parents' prescription drug abuse.

The fat man stood there above the old man's body and told Terry that the old man used to pray on the bus. The fat man said the old man always brought along his old, leather-bound Bible and often read verses that struck him as important or relevant to anyone who'd listened on the bus. Terry remembered watching that fat man blubber for that crushed little old man, and he remembered leaning in close and pointing across the road at the sidewalk on the other side. A small black, leather-bound Bible sat just off the sidewalk near the drain. Terry leaned in close to the fat man and told him all that praying didn't stop the bus.

"Good afternoon, Sgt. Polk," Terry said into the phone in the church's foyer.

"Terry, get your ass over to Majestic Rentals over in Stanton. We gotta situation and everybody's tied up with that wreck up by the Sky Bridge. Some professor from UK and his girlfriend have been staying out in Daniel Boone National Forest doing some study of ferns or something. This professor, he says his mother was murdered over in Hardin County, and he thinks it was because of a book on evolution and science he had published. This professor, a Dr. Kevin Ballard, thinks that the person that killed his mother because of that book might have taken or harmed his girlfriend, one Katherine 'Kate' Johnson." Sgt. Polk didn't sound impressed.

Terry wasn't surprised; Polk had been there since Terry had been in diapers. Nothing surprised a man that entrenched in police work.

"Dr. Ballard said he has asked his friend, one Jason Kinders, to check their apartments in Lexington, and this Mr. Kinders is now on his way to check out the cabin as well."

"Hardin County? Is that Post 4?" Terry asked.

"You know damn well it is. I've confirmed that one Evelyn Ballard is deceased. I've left messages for the shift supervisor and investigative detective. We'll have to go by what this professor says until we hear otherwise," Sgt. Polk said.

"Yessir." Terry cracked the door and watched Abi twiddle her little thumbs while the congregation sat with bowed heads and whispering lips.

"Listen, Terry. There's something about all of this

that I don't like. I can't quite put my finger on it right now, but you watch yourself out there. The sheriff's department said they're sending someone, but you know how that goes. I'll send out the green-ear at shift change," Sgt. Polk said.

"It might be because it's a bit familiar, sir."

"What do you mean?"

"I went out there on that Whitaker homicide, remember?"

There was a pause, some clicking and clinking noises as the sergeant used his computer.

"Ah," he said. "And you let me just carry on about it just now?"

"I didn't want to interrupt, sir."

"Get your ass out there, Terry."

The line went dead.

Terry hung up the phone and stood there, peering through the crack of the door at his daughter. If he'd been a religious man, Terry might've called the sick feeling in his stomach a premonition. David Terry was not a religious man though. He waited until a chorus of Amens sounded and slid back through the door. He dropped back onto the pew and pulled Abigail onto his lap. Quietly into her ear, Terry told her he had to go to work and that he'd see her tomorrow sometime. He said he'd bring her a surprise. Abigail's face rounded with the smile of promises, and Terry kissed her once on the cheek before leaving the church.

Terry had worked Rowan County for the last four years but switched over to Wolfe and Powell because Francine had moved out there with Abi. He lived in a small apartment down from the Wolfe County Library in Stanton, the county seat, where Francine and Abi also resided, though in a two-story brick house near the school. Terry wanted to be as close to Abigail as possible, albeit without having to live with Francine again. He caught himself saying things like "that had been a colossal mistake" often, and he'd stop himself. Abigail came out of his relationship with Francine, despite however sour it went, and Abi was the crux in which Terry tried to arrange his life.

Terry left the church, went home to change, and was on the way to Stanton in ten minutes flat.

****

Kinders had stopped in Stanton for gas. He didn't know if he'd see another gas station after he got off the Mountain Parkway and descended into the Daniel Boone National Forest. The pump was prepay only. He slid his credit card into the pump and lifted the nozzle. He started the gas and walked back to the driver's side door and grabbed the cellphone out of the cup holder.

He tried Kate's cell phone again. It went to voice mail, but he didn't leave a message.

Kinders called Ballard. "I'm in Stanton. I had to stop and get gas, but I should be at the cabin in half an hour or so. Have you heard anything?" Kinders asked.

"No. I'm just now passing through Lexington. I tried calling KSP again, but they stuck me on hold," Ballard said.

The gas pump clicked and stopped. Kinders walked over and, with the phone cradled on his shoulder, returned the nozzle to the pump. "I'm not sure I'll have reception after this point, so are you sure you want me to go on to the cabin by myself and not wait on the police?" Kinders asked.

"I'm sure. The sooner someone can get there, the

A.S. Coomer

better. Maybe she fell and hurt herself or maybe the cabin will have telltale signs of a struggle. God, I hope she's all right," Ballard said.

Kinders got off the phone and pulled out of the station, which was nearly a quarter of a mile off the highway, passing several small businesses and fast food restaurants. Kinders saw a police cruiser in the parking lot of a storefront whose sign read: Majestic Rentals.

He pulled back onto the Mountain Parkway, nearly getting crushed by a coal truck in the process. Kinders honked his horn and flipped the inconsiderate asshole off before slowing down and watching for the exit. Kinders checked the rearview and saw a gray police cruiser flying up behind him. He checked his speed and saw that he wasn't speeding. The cop cut over into the fast lane and accelerated past Kinders and back into the right lane.

"Jesus," Kinders said.

Kinders watched the police vehicle, nearly a mile ahead of him already, take the next exit and disappear down the ramp. Kinders saw the sign for Natural Bridge and took the same exit. He pulled off the ramp and looked both ways, but the cop was gone. He sat there for a minute and checked to see if he had cellphone reception. He did but only barely. It would probably drop the call if he tried to make one. He turned right and passed signs for the Kentucky Reptile Zoo, then the Reptile Zoo itself, and on down the winding road to the Red Tin Cabin.

****

"Should I be worried about my property?" Joan Richards of Majestic Rentals asked.

"I'm not sure, ma'am," Terry said, not bothering to

glance up from the layout of the Red Tin Cabin.

Terry couldn't remember much about the place, so he called the real estate lady and had her meet him at her office. It was a cabin with a loft bedroom and an unfinished basement. There were windows on each side of the building.

"I tried calling them the other day to see if they needed any fresh linens or toilet paper, that sort of thing, but nobody answered. I tried both numbers she left for me. One was to a biological lab or something at UK. The other was the lady's cell phone, and it went to voice mail," Joan said.

"I have your permission to enter the premises, right?" he asked. The sentence may have technically been a question, but there was nothing but certainty in his tone.

"Sure," Joan said. "Are they making meth or something?"

"Can I have the spare key? It'll save me the trouble of kicking the door down," Terry said. "If it comes to it."

"She said they were scientists." The word sounded dirty when the woman said it.

She walked over to her messy desk, opened a drawer, and pulled out a keychain ad for Majestic Rentals.

He looked at each of the brochures for the place and several photos on the woman's computer. There really wasn't a way to sneak up on the place. If you drove, you'd have to get across the creek, then up and around the ridge, all of which would be in sight for anyone on the ridge. If you were standing anywhere in that little valley, you would hear the gravel crunching under the tires, not to mention the splashing of the creek and whatever else ended up being in the path.

If you tried to sneak up on the house on foot, you'd have to do it from behind the Red Tin, which would go up Miller Ridge, past the meat processing plant, and pick your way across the ridge without a trail. You'd have to pray that whoever was on the ridge or in the Red Tin wasn't looking that way because there wouldn't be squat to hide behind.

She gave Terry the key, and he thanked her for her cooperation and left.

He got back onto the Mountain Parkway, heading east, out of Stanton. He entered Natural Bridge State Park and turned off, onto Natural Bridge Road. The road bobbed and weaved through the hills and the trees, and he felt like a boxer, knowing exactly when to cut the wheel and when to let up on the gas or hammer it on down. He knew the area fairly well already, even though he hadn't really had many calls out this way before he was promoted; this one was the second he went out on in the area as a detective, the first being the Whitaker homicide.

Terry launched the cruiser across the creek, up and around the hills onto the ridge. The Red Tin Cabin stood shining in the afternoon sun. He pulled the cruiser nearly up to the door. There wasn't another car anywhere on the ridge. Terry sat behind the wheel for a moment, watching the place. He couldn't tell if there were any lights on inside, and he didn't see any movement.

He radioed Post and told them he'd arrived at the Red Tin Cabin and was preparing to knock on the door. He stepped out of the car and, with one hand on the butt of his pistol, approached the front door of the cabin. He beat the bottom of his left hand on the door, three loud knocks.

"Kentucky State Police," Terry yelled.

He slowed his breathing, cocked his head to the right, and listened. A woodpecker hammered away on a tree nearby. A car horn sounded from some distance beyond the cabin. Terry didn't hear anything from inside.

He knocked three more times, harder this go around.

"This is Detective Terry. Open the door," he said. "Miss Johnson, open the door."

There was no reply. He moved his hand to his pocket to retrieve the spare key, but he stopped and put his hand on the door knob instead. The knob twisted and clicked. Then the door swung open.

Terry drew his Smith & Wesson 1076 and stepped into the darkened interior of the Red Tin. The sunshine outside made it seem darker than it was. He felt around on the wall beside the door and flicked on the lights.

"Police. Is anybody home?" Terry called out, sweeping by the dinner table into the living room. He checked the bathroom, small closet, kitchen and loft, but all were empty. He opened the door onto the back porch. The hot tub was covered; the deck chairs were empty. He lifted the hot tub cover and checked underneath it. Nothing.

Terry walked around the cabin back to the front. He radioed Post and told them the place was empty. Then walked back inside.

****

Terry stood in the doorway of the bathroom,

looking at the water-covered floor. A towel sat folded on the closed lid of the toilet by the bathtub. Several candles had been lit but had burned themselves out. Thick piles of melted wax sat on the floor underneath the window, the sink, and the left side of the tub. The tub's drain cover was of the pushdown variety; you push down to close and push again to open. Terry saw that it was pushed down, closing the drain, so somebody could take a bath. Soap scum covered the bottom and sides of the tub; the water had drained slowly on its own.

Someone's bath had been interrupted.

From the bathroom doorway looking in, Terry imagined the tub full of hot, soapy water, the glow of candles on the walls and a woman submerged up to her neck. Terry looked at the back of her head. He took two steps into the room and was directly behind her.

"She didn't have a chance," Terry said.

****

Kinders found the road and stopped before the creek. He left his car running, opened the door and walked over to it.

"You gotta be fucking kidding me," Kinders said, dropping to his haunches before the slow-moving water.

He picked up a rock and tossed it in. He could see the bottom. The creek couldn't be more than six inches deep, but still, it was a fucking creek and right in the middle of what he assumed *these* people thought was a road.

Kinders walked back over to his car and shut the door.

"The things we do for friends," Kinders said and

sighed. "You owe me big time, Ballard."

He eased the car forward and crossed the creek, holding his breath.

He navigated around, up, and over the ridge to find a Kentucky State Police squad car sitting in front of what he thought must be the Red Tin Cabin.

"Shit," he said and killed the engine.

Before he could open the door, a stocky man emerged from the darkness of the open front door. The man stepped out with his hand on the butt of the gun he wore on his hip.

Kinders raised both of his hands, a sign of his harmlessness. The man walked to the car. He had closely cropped hair, and the moonlight shone off his scalp as he approached.

"Keep your hands where I can see 'em," the man said a few steps from the door with his hand still on his gun.

"I'm Jason Kinders, a friend of Ballard's. He called me and asked me to see if Kate was okay," Kinders said.

The man reached down and opened the car door and motioned Kinders out. Kinders got out with his hands still in the air.

"Driver's license," the man demanded.

"You gonna write me a parking ticket or something?" Kinders said. He cringed as the words flew from his lips. *Mouth moves faster than your brain, boy.* He reached back for his wallet and handed his license over. "Is she in there?" Kinders asked.

The man studied the license and spoke into his radio. He walked around Kinders' car and read the license plate into the receiver, then returned it to his belt.

Several awkward moments passed; then a woman's voice mumbled out of the walkie talkie's speaker. The man nodded his head in affirmation, then walked back over to Kinders.

"I'm Detective David Terry with the Kentucky State Police. Where's Kevin Ballard and Katherine Johnson?"

Kinders shook his head and said, "Ballard's on the way here, and neither of us know where Kate is. That's why I'm here. Ballard called me and told me somebody murdered his mom, and he thinks this person took Kate, too, maybe killed her."

Those last three words came out in a whisper.

Det. Terry and Jason Kinders stood in front of the Red Tin, listening to the sound of an approaching vehicle.

Without warning, Det. Terry shoved Jason Kinders to the side, putting the police car between him and the driveway. He knelt beside him and drew his pistol.

"Oh, Jesus," Kinders said.

"Stay down until I say otherwise," Det. Terry said.

Kevin Ballard's navy-blue SUV came flying up the drive. He locked the brakes and cut the steering wheel to the left, hard. He just barely missed Jason Kinders' rear bumper.

"It's Ballard. It's Ballard," Kinders told Det. Terry, rising to his feet.

Kevin jumped out of the vehicle and practically ran over to the two men.

"Det. Terry, thank God you're here," Ballard said.

"She's not here," Det. Terry said, pointing to the open cabin door.

The sun had long since gone down, but the heat had barely abated, and Kinders' skin was slick with sweat.

Ballard stopped in mid-stride toward the cabin door. He turned back to Det. Terry and Kinders.

"There's not…" Ballard paused, his voice low. "There's not any blood or anything, is there?"

Det. Terry shook his head and spoke into his walkie talkie.

****

There wasn't much for the police to go on. A bathtub that had drained slowly and a wet floor. They looked for fingerprints but were not successful and weren't expecting to be. The police took pictures and documented what they saw in the cabin, which wasn't much. The Middlefork Fire and Rescue team arrived and worked with the police in setting up a search area, which ended up being about a four-mile radius around the Red Tin Cabin, as the sun began its slow decline.

Kevin was told that Kate had probably set out for a hike and gotten herself lost. She would more than likely turn up in the next few hours. This sort of thing happened all the time; he shouldn't worry. But Kevin worried.

Some of the other officers posited that she might've wanted to get away for a little R&R. When Kevin argued that she would've told him, they gave him sidelong looks that said, "Maybe she wanted some *alone* time, bub."

Again, they told him not to worry, but he couldn't help it.

The police released a statement to the press with Kate's description that requested anybody with information regarding her whereabouts to contact them immediately. Volunteers began descending upon the secluded cabin, and Kevin got the feeling that the place was the host of some ancient tent revival. A bastion of light in the darkened wilderness, sending out men and women with flashlights to battle the darkness, to search out and return a child of the light to the lighthouse.

A K-9 search and rescue crew arrived, and the dogs' handlers handled Kate's clothes, clean and not. The dogs sniffed and salivated all over her clothes, and several smaller more intimate articles were placed in plastic bags to remind the dogs of the scent of the person they were seeking.

Kevin answered question after question, a barrage of whens and wheres.

"When was the last time you had communication with her?"

"Friday afternoon before leaving to visit my mother for the weekend."

"Did she have any plans of leaving the cabin?"

"No. She said she was tired of hiking and was going to 'veg-out' the entire weekend. She planned on watching a lot of television and reading. She brought along the *Lord of the Rings* trilogy. She said she'd never read the books, just saw the movies."

"What was she wearing the last time you saw her?"

"She was still in her hiking gear. She probably threw them in the basket in the corner of the bathroom. She was going to take a bath and put on her pajamas. She said she didn't plan on wearing anything other than her pajamas all weekend."

A man from the state police and another from the sheriff's department gave Kevin an outline of the process. LKP (last known position) had been established as the Red Tin Cabin. SAR (search and rescue) teams were being assembled for the next few days, and hasty teams were being sent out first. At Kevin's puzzled looks, it was further explained that hasty teams were sent out first—while SAR teams were being culled together—to search the area as quickly as possible, focusing on the areas she'd be most liable to be. If the hasty teams didn't find her, they would then organize grid search teams, which would consist of whomever they could get out there to help. With the grid team, everyone would line up and comb every inch of the search area.

Kevin felt ignorant. He had his PhD but knew next to nothing about any of this. He felt like a lost child being pulled along by a helpful stranger. He was told there was absolutely nothing he could do at the moment but wait.

He sat on the couch in the Red Tin with the front door open, bugs flying in and out as they pleased. He watched Kate's face pop up on the evening news. He was informed by the newscaster to call the Kentucky State Police or Wolfe County Sheriff's Department with any information on her whereabouts and that volunteers were needed for a search party.

Kevin looked at the phone, expecting it to ring. It didn't.

****

They ended the search around four in the morning. It was to resume at nine am at the Red Tin Cabin. Kevin was informed that several men on horseback would aid in the search in the morning and the K-9 unit would continue their search as well. The state police, sheriffs, firemen, and volunteers cleared out. The great luminous tent revival ended, and a thick blanket of darkness settled around the cabin.

Kevin Ballard and Jason Kinders were left standing in the brightly lit kitchen.

"What do we do now?" Kevin asked.

Kinders shook his head. "I don't know."

"There was water on the floor and soap in the tub. She'd been taking a bath but had to leave quickly," Kevin said.

"Or she was taken," Kinders said.

They shared an uncomfortable glance.

"I know you don't want to hear it but look at it. She drew a bathtub for herself, left a towel on the toilet right there next to the tub but didn't use it. There's water all over the floor. It looks to me that somebody must've snuck in and surprised her when she was in the tub," Kinders said.

Kevin walked out of the kitchen and into the bathroom; Kinders didn't follow him. Kevin stood momentarily in the doorway before going on in. He sat down on the closed toilet and stared blankly into the tub. He reached a hand into the tub and let his forefinger drag the bottom, on up the sides. Kevin brought the finger to his face, it was white with dried soap. It smelt like lavender.

Chapter Eight

Kinders took the couch, and Kevin slept on the bed in the loft of the Red Tin. Kevin lay awake for hours, hearing whispers amid the crickets' stridulations and faint moans under the echoing calls of the owls. It was late into the early morning hours before dawn when Kevin found his sleep. It came slowly but took him down deep.

****

The black cloth stuck to his skin and itched as he walked. Kevin stopped periodically to peel it off his sweating back. Kevin walked in between rows and rows of Mammoth sunflowers that stood towering over him, occasionally blocking the glaring sun. He didn't know where he was or where he was going.

Kevin cut through the rows of sunflowers, pushing aside the plants just far enough for him to slip between and let the flowers fall back into place with a susurrus brushing of the petals and leaves.

The moments stretched out like decades; time had no real meaning. Kevin walked under the watchful eyes of sunflowers and their god: the bulbous shining sun. The crisp blue sky hung cloudless and unchanging, but the flowered heads of the plants turned and followed Kevin's passing. He walked and walked until the sun fell. It slumped behind the wooded top of a rolling knob as Kevin finally emerged from the field of sunflowers.

A man was hunched over a small campfire, his back to Kevin. The moon had taken the night sky and filled it with resplendent crystals, twinkling diamonds in the darkness. The heat of the sun was gone, the chill of night blanketed all. The man's back jerked and moved as his hands and arms worked at the fire.

Kevin swept back into the sunflowers and followed them around the clearing to the foot of the mountain. The firelight flickered off his eyes, and for a moment, the man's head jerked up in Kevin's direction. The man could not discern between Kevin's blond hair and the blond tint of the sunflowers in the firelight.

The man turned his head back to his work and Kevin watched. The man pulled out thick, long sticks from a wooden box to his left. He took out the sticks and laid them around the fire, careful not to catch them alight. He'd lay three or four of the sticks parallel to the fire, then warm his hands close to the flames. He dragged the box around the fire as he surrounded it with the cylindrical sticks.

From his vantage point, hidden behind the Mammoth sunflowers, Kevin could not clearly see the man's face or the sanguine sticks he handled with such revered carefulness, but he thought them candles, the kind they used in the great cathedrals of the superstitious past. Kevin squinted over the shimmering heat of the fire and saw that the man's mouth was working. He craned his ears out into the night and heard the night's sounds. Among them, the crackling of the fire, and then just barely discernible was the low, melodic drawl of the candle man.

"Didn't mean no harm," the singsong candle man said. "No, sir. No harm t'all."

The candle man set three more candles around the fire and cautiously reached back into the wooden box, where his hand groped about but came back empty. The man turned and, with both hands resting on the top of the box, peered inside. Kevin watched the man's facial expression change comically from revulsion to satisfaction.

"She's empty. Lord, yes, she's empty," the candle man said.

He rose to his feet, stretched, and ran his hands along the small of his back.

"Couldn't have come any sooner neither. Back's gonna give out on me soon enough," the candle man said, walking to the candles on the other side of the fire that he'd pulled from the wooden box first.

The man dropped back to his knees and set about rolling the candles over in the dirt like frying sausages in a pan.

"I caint help it. A man caint sleep with 'em sitting right in there by his bed. Jus' a waitin' to go," the candle man clapped his hands together loudly.

"Boom," he said, his hands returning to the candles, turning the sticks over in the dirt.

Sound and movement tore Kevin's eyes from the candle man toward the foot of the mountain. He noticed a different shade of dark there then. The mouth of a tunnel yawned into the starlit night and the sound of men echoed from within.

****

The dancing beam of light flickered on the inner walls of the tunnel. It grew brighter and the dancing drifted along the walls until it met the open air of darkness where it fell to the ground that the men walked on.

"Jesus Christ! You ain't got it thawed out yet?" a tall man in overalls said, his breath clouding before him.

He carried a large tin lantern, a flame ducking and rising with each of his steps. Behind him followed two more men in overalls, one of whom also carried a lantern. The lanternless man kept his hands buried deep in his pockets.

The candle man climbed up onto his feet and dusted off the knees of his overalls.

"Almost there," the candle man replied, the tone of his voice supplicating.

"The goddamn *sun* is almost here," the lantern man said.

"I didn't mean no harm. I didn't think it could freeze. Something made a fire, didn't seem right that it could just freeze right up like it did," the candle man said, hunkering down a little lower with each step the lantern men took.

"I didn't know you *could* think. If we don't get started, 'fore long, we'll be digging this goddamn hole on through winter. You know how heavy rock feels in the winter?" the lantern man said.

The lantern light and the light of the campfire bled into one another.

"I jus' couldn't sleep with 'em in the cabin there with me. Just waitin' to go off in the middle of the night. I didn't want to wake up dead, that's all," the candle man said, dropping back down to his knees before the lantern man.

The candle man busied himself with turning the sticks over in the light of the fire. An ember popped up into the cold night air and waved briefly before falling onto one of the sanguine dynamite sticks Kevin had somehow mistaken for candles.

The world erupted into hot flashes of white and crackling yellow, then thundered into low rumbles and groans of red. Kevin sat upright in the loft bed of the Red Tin covered in sweat just as the morning sun crept over the rolling hills beyond the ridge.

****

That first morning back at the Red Tin, with Kinders asleep on the couch in the living room, Kevin called Kate's phone. It rang once in his ear, and Kevin couldn't help but sit up in the bed and listen for it to ring somewhere in the cabin.

It didn't.

The call quietly clicked over to Kate's voice mail, and Kevin felt his stomach drop, the first plummet of a rollercoaster. He did his best to deaden the sound of his sadness, but he heard it echo faintly in the cedar cabin.

****

On the couch in the living room, Kinders lay somewhere between sleep and waking, hearing Kate's cries for mercy.

****

Terry knocked on the Red Tin Cabin's door at nine-thirty that morning. The search party had already assembled and descended into the woods on both sides of the ravine. The sun was dissipating most of the morning mist, but the drive to the cabin had been eerily fog covered. When the cruiser peaked the hill, the Red Tin shone in the morning light like some mirage of tranquility.

Ballard let him in and poured him a cup of coffee.

A.S. Coomer

His friend and colleague from UK was there as well. Neither man looked like he had had much sleep.

"What do we do now?" Ballard asked.

Terry took a sip from his coffee, then set the cup on the table.

"If there's a ransom, we'll hear from them today," Terry told them.

He watched both of their facial expressions closely, looking for any sign. Kinders looked over at Ballard, then back at Terry, then at his hands in his lap. Ballard looked to Terry, then out of the front window, at the parked vehicles.

"That didn't tell me what I needed to do," Ballard said.

"You don't do nothing. You sit here, keep your cell phone charged, and the landline free. You check in with me on my cell every hour on the hour and don't do anything without talking to me," Terry said.

"I can't just sit here. Shouldn't I be out combing the hills or screaming through a megaphone or handing out fliers? Something?" Ballard looked on the verge of more tears; his already red eyes welled, but he wiped them before they could fall.

****

The sun filled the cabin with light late into the evening. Then it sank below, somewhere west, and the shadows flooded into the Red Tin. Kevin and Kinders went about turning on every light they could. Each stood and went about the task with not a word shared between them. They'd passed most of the day in silence. Sitting on the couch, at the dinner table, on the front or back porches. Waiting and hoping and drinking cup after cup, then pot after pot, of black coffee.

Kevin called Det. Terry every hour on the hour as instructed, but there were no new leads, no new information. Kate remained gone; Kevin's mother and father remained dead, and he sat in a small, cedar cabin with someone he wouldn't have considered a friend a week ago.

After every light had been turned on, Kevin and Kinders sat down on the couch and turned on the television. Kevin flipped through the channels twice before settling for a rerun of some 90s sitcom. He stared at the familiar characters, people he'd allowed into his home for years, but he couldn't pay them a bit of attention. He watched them move about in their house, their work, their bar, the stages in the set's lot somewhere thousands of miles away.

Kevin walked into the kitchen and picked up his cell phone, which was charging on the counter. There were no missed calls or text messages. He opened up his email and absently scrolled through the departmental nugatory before returning the phone to its place on the counter and climbing the stairs to the loft.

He sat down on the bed and called down to Kinders that he was going to take a nap and that his cell phone was on the counter if it rang.

Kevin pulled off his shoes, then his shirt, and sank back onto the pillows. He lay there a moment, then reached over, and turned off the bedside lamp on the side he usually slept on, the left. He rolled over on his stomach and reached across to Kate's bedside lamp and pulled the chain. He let his arm drop across Kate's pillows and lay there, diagonal across the bed, and slept on top of the covers.

****

The minutes were years and the seconds decades. The robe itched, and he was sweating under the glaring sun. The sunflowers seemed closer and closer until he felt he walked in a flowering tunnel. They turned their petal eyes down on him, and he felt them breathe. He'd been running, but now he was in the clearing, at the foot of the mountain, watching the candle man thaw out the dynamite. He opened his mouth to yell. Then a stick was sparked, and everything was white and yellow and hot and rumbling.

Then there was the darkness and a voice filling it, telling him that he "didn't mean no harm." He didn't think something made of fire could freeze, that he thought of it like ice. Ice couldn't be left out in the sun and burst into flames, so why should something made from fire be able to freeze? The question jangled around in his head until Kevin heard Kinders call his name from downstairs.

Kevin sat bolt upright in the middle of the bed, swaying, shaking the sleep off like a wet dog.

"Ballard, Detective Terry just called. He's on his way over," Kinders called up the stairs of the loft into the darkness.

"Good," Kevin said, pulling the lamp's chain and squinting into the light.

****

Terry didn't trust Dr. Kevin Ballard. It didn't seem too far stretched to suppose that Dr. Ballard was emotionally unstable and had killed the girl at the gas station, his mother at his house, and his girlfriend at the cabin. Those who preach religion don't really believe it; those that shout out against it need it the most. That's what his grandfather used to say. David Terry's

Pentecostal mother, God rest her soul, used to call her father-in-law, his grandfather, lazy and said that he said things like that to justify his laziness.

Terry had spent the morning on the phone with Det. Wesley Conner of Post 4. Det. Conner was assigned the Evelyn Ballard case as well as the Angela Rogers case. He didn't think the two were connected. Det. Conner said Angela Rogers looked to be a suicide and Evelyn Ballard a murder. Terry pointed out the similarity of their deaths, deeply slit wrists, but Det. Conner said he had an unstable former foster child just getting over the trauma of her first abortion and life on her own as an adult. Det. Conner had that one all but written up, despite the fact that both Evelyn Ballard and Angela Rogers had been murdered relatively close, and Dr. Kevin Ballard's alibi put him on the road for several hours, well within the time frame of both murders. Dr. Ballard's alibi relied on Katherine Johnson, who was the last person he spoke to before hitting the road to visit his mother.

The bodies just kept piling up around this Dr. Kevin Ballard. Evelyn Ballard, Angela Rogers, Larry Whitaker, and probably Katherine "Kate" Johnson as well. Terry felt like there was something glaringly obvious sitting somewhere in the foreground of the painting, but he couldn't find it.

Sgt. Polk didn't act like he believed Ballard either but wouldn't admit it. Polk told Terry to look into "every possible avenue." He didn't specifically name Ballard, but he didn't have to; he knew Terry would walk down each and every street until he pulled onto the avenue he was looking for.

Terry pulled up to the Red Tin Cabin and knocked

on the door. Jason Kinders answered and let him in, then yelled up into the loft, letting Ballard know that he was there. Ballard came down the stairs, adjusting his pants and shirt, his hair showed that he had been sleeping.

"Afternoon, Dr. Ballard," Terry said.

"Do you have any news?" Ballard asked, sitting down at the table.

Terry pulled out a chair and sat down. "No," he said. "Have you heard anything today?"

"Nothing," Ballard said, holding Terry's stare.

Jason Kinders plopped down into a chair and said, "What's the next move, Detective?"

Ballard and Terry both turned to Kinders, as if they expected him to answer the question himself.

"Unless either of you have any information you may have forgotten to tell me," Terry said, looking from Kinders to Ballard, "we wait while the search continues."

****

The phone rang. Kevin had fallen asleep in the armchair in the living room. He sat up, shook off the sleep, and, in the blue glow of the muted television, walked past the couch where Kinders lay, into the kitchen, where his cell phone sat on the counter, charging.

It was Aunt Bonnie. Kevin sighed and answered the call.

"Any luck?" she asked.

Kevin checked his watch: 9:45 pm.

"No. No luck. No word from Kate. No word from the psychopath either," Kevin said, rubbing crust from his eyes.

He tried to take the phone to the table and sit down, but the charging cord wasn't long enough. He reached over, pulled a chair from the table, and sat at the counter.

Aunt Bonnie rattled on about the letters, phone calls, and visits of condolence she'd received since she'd been staying at Kevin's parents' house in Hardin County. She said a reporter from the *News-Enterprise* had left several messages for Kevin. Aunt Bonnie said she'd even taken a message from a man with the *Louisville Courier-Journal* who wanted to interview Kevin about his mother's death, as well as the Angela Rogers death at a gas station in Sonora on the same night.

Kevin listened and made utterances of affirmation and understanding. He sat with his head bowed and his eyes closed, one hand holding the phone to his ear, the other massaging the bridge of his nose.

Aunt Bonnie stopped talking for a moment, and Kevin heard her swallow, then clear her throat.

Kevin opened his eyes.

"Kevin, a man from the state police came by today. He said he needs to talk to you," Aunt Bonnie said.

"What did he say he wanted to talk about, Aunt Bonnie?" Kevin asked, sitting up in the chair.

"I'm not really sure, Kevin. He asked where you were and when you would be home. He asked how to get a hold of you and if you had a cell phone or a phone where you were that he could reach you," Aunt Bonnie said.

Kevin heard her swallow again.

"I gave him your cell phone number and the number to the cabin. I hope you're not mad at me,

Kevin. He was real serious and insistent, and I didn't want to make it seem like I, or you, had anything to hide or had done anything wrong," Aunt Bonnie said.

She took a deep breath after having shot out all of it in a rush like a kid throwing back his head, swallowing all the medicine as quickly as possible, to get it over with.

Kevin didn't know what to make of it. He thought back to Det. Terry's visit earlier that afternoon. Det. Terry didn't have any new information or leads, but he had still come to the Red Tin. Was he just checking to make sure Kevin hadn't fled? Did the police think he had something to do with Kate's disappearance? His mother's murder? The murder of the girl at the gas station, which the paper reported as a suicide? Kevin had seen the weekday crime dramas; they all said that, ninety-nine percent of the time, it was the husband or boyfriend that was at the root of it all.

He was silent for a moment, thinking that over, when he saw it.

In the center of the front door's window, the green of the orangumantis necklace projected itself against the darkness of the night behind.

He let the phone drop from his hand and clatter onto the table. He walked over to the front door and turned on the floodlights. He opened the door and looked out into the darkness around the rim of light from the floodlights. He didn't see anybody.

He stepped out on the porch and pulled the door to. Kate's orangumantis on the thin gold chain hung from a small blued lath nail, probably used to hold Christmas wreaths and the like, just above the window. It spun slightly in a small concentric circle from the opening and closing of the door. Kevin pulled the necklace from the nail and watched it turn before his eyes.

Kinders opened the door and stepped out onto the porch with Kevin's cell phone in his hand.

"It's your aunt, Ballard," Kinders said, reaching the phone out to Kevin. "What is that?"

"He's been here," Kevin said, watching the orangumatis slowly turn.

****

After he finished railing Kevin about handling evidence and how detrimental it could be to a case, Det. Terry asked him when he noticed the necklace.

"Nine-forty-five. I fell asleep in the living room in the chair, and my phone rang. It was my aunt Bonnie. She wanted to brief me on who came by and expressed their condolences for my mother's passing, that sort of thing. I answered the call here in the kitchen, where my cell phone was charging on the counter. I sat down in the chair right here," Kevin said, pulling it into the center of the kitchen. "Then, I looked up and saw it there in the window. The green just stood out."

Det. Terry held the resealable plastic bag up to his eyes and looked at the small green animal on the gold chain.

"What in God's name is it?" Det. Terry asked.

A smile crept across Kevin's face, the first one in days. "It's an orangumantis. A cross between a praying mantis and an orangutan," Kevin said.

"And you're sure it's Katherine Johnson's?" Det. Terry asked.

Kevin nodded his head. "I found it on the Internet and bought it for her just a few months back. It's kind of an inside joke. See, we teach several intro biology classes at UK and also go out to middle schools and high schools and give lectures on evolutionary biology. It never fails that we have one person, sometimes jokingly, sometimes not, ask us something along the lines of 'If evolution is real, why aren't there crocoducks or ligers or minotaurs or orangumantises?' It's hearing that question after you gave them a general rundown on the diversity of species, adaptation, and natural selection that is so frustrating. I've been doing it for a few years now, but Kate just started, so I thought I'd go ahead and give her her baptism of fire and let her wear it around her neck," Kevin said.

Det. Terry lowered the bag and looked at Kevin.

"And this hadn't been here or in your possession since Katherine Johnson's disappearance?" Det. Terry asked.

Kevin didn't like the tone of Detective Terry's voice or the direction of his questioning. There was no trace of the smile on Kevin's face now. "No. I haven't had the necklace this whole time nor has it been in my possession since first gifting it to Kate." Kevin did not hide his rankle.

Det. Terry turned toward Jason Kinders, standing just inside the door frame.

"And what about you, Mr. Kinders?" Det. Terry asked. "Have you seen this before?"

Det. Terry held the bag up for Kinders to see.

"I saw it tonight after Ballard found it on the door, and I remember seeing it a few times over the past couple of months on Kate," Kinders said, glancing over at Kevin.

Kevin thought he saw a bit of shame in the look, as if Kinders felt bad recalling sneaking peeks at Kate's breasts, as if it somehow made him dirty now that she was gone.

****

No fingerprints could be lifted off the necklace or the chain, but they sent it off to the lab for further examination anyway. It was doubtful anything would come from it. They tried the front door of the Red Tin Cabin as well but weren't able to identify any solid fingerprints near the nail. There was a hodgepodge of fingerprints on the knob but nothing new to go off of.

Terry had asked Dr. Kevin Ballard to come into the station, which Terry called *the office*, for "routine questioning." Terry wanted to get Ballard on camera and shake his cage to see what might rattle out. Ballard was not a happy camper when Terry made his request.

"What the fuck? Am I a suspect to you?" Ballard had screamed into the phone.

Terry took a sip from the cold cup of coffee and skimmed through the pdf of an article in the *News-Enterprise*, the paper out of Elizabethtown over in Hardin County. The paper had used Angela Rogers's senior portrait, and the headline had read *Area Troubled Teen Meets Untimely End*. The article informed the reader that Angela Rogers had lived a rough life, according to her former foster mother. She had struggled with drug addiction, sexual and physical abuse, and suicidal ideations, and was found dead at her place of employment, the BP in Sonora. The article read that the video surveillance of the gas station was not operational, and there had been no eye-witnesses. The article said a customer had found her behind the register with both wrists slit. The investigation was ongoing, but the police were operating under the assumption that Rogers's death was a suicide.

Terry closed the screen and opened another pdf, this one concerning Evelyn Ballard. The article said Evelyn Ballard had been murdered in her home in rural Hardin County by an unknown assailant. According to the article, the police were asking anyone with information regarding the incident to report it immediately. The article did not give the specifics of Mrs. Ballard's murder or mention anything about the message left on the wall, which had been written in the victim's blood.

Could Dr. Kevin Ballard have killed his mother? Did he play in her blood? Terry wondered. *Is he using this religious insanity ploy to shift the blame to someone else?*

****

When Kevin Ballard arrived at the station, he was not alone. A short, balding man in a suit and tie accompanied him. Ballard introduced the man, one Ronald Wright, as an attorney and friend. Terry didn't think Ballard would bring in an attorney.

He shook hands with the attorney and led them both to the small interrogation room where he left them for a few minutes. Terry went into the room adjacent and looked into the one-sided mirror at Ballard and Wright. Sgt. Polk sat at a chair, looking into the room.

"He brought an attorney," Polk said.

"Yes, he did. Ronald Wright. Have you heard of him?" Terry asked, watching the two men try to get comfortable in the chairs on the other side of the mirror.

"No, I haven't. I looked him up after Martha signed the both of them in, though. He has represented Dr. Kevin Ballard and the University of Kentucky Press on several copyright and intellectual property cases regarding Dr. Ballard's work and a couple of real right-wing Christian fundamentalists," Polk said.

"Hmm. I wonder why he felt the need to have Mr. Wright with him today?" Det. Terry asked.

"I wonder," Polk said.

Terry joined Dr. Kevin Ballard and the Honorable Ronald Wright in the small, brightly lit interrogation room.

****

"Did you get along with your mother?" Det. Terry asked, folding his hands together on the table.

Kevin's brow furrowed. "Of course. What kind of question is that?"

"So you two wouldn't have any reason to fight?"

"I'm not sure I understand what you're asking me here."

"Was it about your work? Did she not agree with you? What about your book?" Det. Terry asked, leaning forward.

"What does any of that have to do with my mother?" Kevin asked, but his face betrayed him. He looked away at the corner of the table.

"You tell me," Det. Terry said. He sat back in his chair, his hands still interlocked on the table.

Repent, Sinner.

Written in blood over and across the title page of *Nolin & the Hellbenders*, sitting on his bed like the black mask of an executioner. Kevin hadn't told the police in Hardin County about it. He hadn't told anybody about it. He'd kept it in the bottom of the duffle bag and only taken it out at night, holding it in his shaking hands like some pagan blood-magic voodoo doll. Like the instrument of his mother's death. And probably Kate's, too. A shameful, destructive thing.

"How did you find out about it?" Kevin asked, dropping his chin to his chest.

Ron jerked up in his chair, threw an arm around Kevin's shoulder, and turned them both away from the detective and the one-way mirror. "What in God's name are you doing? Are you trying to incriminate yourself in all this horror?" he asked.

Kevin looked at his hands and felt the sweat run down his spine under the cool air of the overhead vent.

****

Terry hid the surprise from his face. He also resisted the urge to shotgun the handful of questions that poised themselves in his head, loaded on his tongue. Terry forced himself to just sit there and stare at Dr. Kevin Ballard, who was about to let something rattle on out of that cage, and the tape was rolling.

Chapter Nine

He'd been gone for most of the days. He left very early in the mornings and arrived with the dusk. He had a lock on the outside of the door that Kate heard him toy with when he left and when he returned, though she never saw the man with any keys.

The man didn't speak to her after that first night. He wouldn't even look at her, which, for some reason, really bothered her. It was like she wasn't really there, just another Appalachian mutt left crated to wallow in its own filth and die. Those first few days, she begged the man to release her, promising she wouldn't press any charges if he just took her to a road, any road, and let her go. He didn't even have to take her into a town, she pleaded.

He didn't even acknowledge the sound of her voice.

Kate switched to making the man promises; she'd do whatever he wanted if he'd let her go. She told him she'd let him do whatever he wanted, anything, if he would just let her go. She talked and begged and cried. Then she screamed and yelled at him, flinging every curse and insult she could come up with, but she got no reaction.

She sat quietly and watched him closely whenever he came into the room now.

He tied a dog collar around her neck that first

morning, and he'd let her outside on a leash to piss and shit in the brush on the left side of the trailer, once in the morning and once at night. She'd lift the oversized T-shirt out of the way and squat down to do her business. Drops of piss and flecks of shit crusted her bare ankles and feet. She tried to wipe them on the brush, but the man jerked the leash each time and pulled her back inside the faded salmon-colored singlewide trailer. He'd take her back to the corner of the living room, where he'd secure the chain into place, then remove the leash, and leave her.

****

She could hear him in the night and see the flicker of candles on the ceiling of the far hall. Whispering and whispering in his slow, quiet voice. She tried to hear every word, but his voice was too soft, and there were walls and doors between them, cheap paneling though they were, but she heard enough to know he was reading from the Bible or some other such religious book. She heard *Lord*, *Almighty*, *God* and the like repeatedly. She also heard the crinkling of pages and the sound of something rough or scratchy moving about paper. Then she'd hear another voice from back there. She'd swear there was another person in the house, speaking quickly and urgently in some language she didn't recognize. She knew no one else was in the trailer other than the two of them, and this scared Kate very much.

****

Everybody knew the Conns or had, at least, heard of them. Seemed like most every place you went to, you ran into a Conn. They'd married, divorced, and had children with almost every other family in the county and several from the surrounding counties.

Terry pulled into the trailer park and watched four skinny teenagers disappear behind some trailers, a thin trail of smoke following them. Somewhere up on the ridge, a dog barked. Inside one of the trailers, a subwoofer bumped out bass.

Terry pulled around to the last row of trailers and stopped in front of a faded seafoam green single-wide with a "7C" beside the door. He honked the horn three times and waited. He listened to several heavy sets of feet stomp about inside. From the far side of the trailer, he heard the sound of a hushed argument, then the flushing of a toilet.

Det. Terry smiled to himself and honked the horn two more times.

The front door of the trailer opened, and a thin woman stepped out onto the small, lopsided porch, and smiled down, toward Terry in the cruiser. Her teeth were heavily yellowed and speckled with black rot. She could have been sixty years old; she could have been thirty.

Terry used the power windows and rolled down the passenger side. He motioned the woman to step down off the porch toward the car.

The woman stepped down onto the mud and gravel, barefooted, and leaned into the window, propping herself up with her right arm. "How are you, Trooper Terry?" the woman said, her voice distant, slow.

"I'm doing just fine, Emily. How are you doing? I hear those children of yours are just a-growing and a-growing," Terry said.

The woman smiled and nodded her head. A thin

blue liquid slid from her nostrils.

"They're a-doin' just fine with them foster parents, there. Ricky got held back last year, but with his ADHD and all, what can you do? Yeah, they're doin' just fine and so are we. Me 'n Dirty have been doin' our parentin' classes and are gonna start substance abuse classes nex' week," Emily said.

Terry motioned to his nose and made a deliberate wiping motion, then pointed at Emily. She blankly watched him, then stood for a second, not understanding. When comprehension dawned on her, she turned her head away from the window and wiped her nose on her shirt sleeve. She looked at it, then wiped it on the short jean shorts she was wearing, but it didn't come off.

"I've got a little bit of a cold," Emily said, turning back to Terry and settling herself back on the window.

"I see that," Terry said. "Who all's staying here with you, Emily?"

Emily turned back toward the trailer as if to see if somebody was standing in the doorway.

"Just me and Dirty now that the kids are in care."

"Would you mind callin' Dirty on out here? I've got some questions for you all," Terry asked and smiled.

"We ain't in no kind of trouble, are we?" Emily asked, her head tilting back on her neck, then sliding back forward.

"No. No, nothing like that, Emily. Just call Dirty out here, so I can ask you all about some things and get out of your hair for the evening," Terry said.

Emily steadied herself on her feet without the support of the car, then stepped up the two steps onto the porch and stuck her head in the front door of the trailer.

"Dirt," Emily called. "Dirt, come up here for a minute. Trooper Terry is here, said he's got some questions to ask us."

Terry heard a lower-pitched, muffled reply, then heavy feet stomping away from the front door to the far side of the trailer, then the sound of the toilet flushing two more times.

Emily stumbled off the porch and propped herself in the passenger side window again. She smiled and wiped her nose with the back of her hand, then turned her head away from the cruiser, hocked a loogie, and spat it on the ground near her bare feet. Emily squinted down at it, saw that it was blue from the Xanax and kicked dirt and gravel over it. Emily was oblivious to the smeared blue on the back of her hand and across her upper lip.

An imposing man appeared in the door and stepped out on the small porch, which groaned under his weight.

"Evening, Trooper Terry," the man said, stepping off the porch.

"How do, Walter?" Terry asked.

"What can we he'p you'ns with?" Walter asked, standing beside Emily.

Terry watched him sway like some lone pine on a strip-mined hill. Walter reached out and steadied himself on the cruiser.

"I'm trying to find JJ, Walter. I've got some questions I need to ask him. I thought maybe you or Emily might know where he was," Terry said, smiling at Walter, then Emily.

Emily turned her head to Walter, who looked down at his bare feet.

"Come on, now. I thought we had us an understanding. I'm not saying I'm going to go out there and bust his head or nothing. I just got some questions I need to ask him, that's all," Terry said, showing Emily and Walter the upturned palms of his hands.

"What if'n we says we don't know where JJ is?" Walter asked, still looking at his feet.

Terry cleared his throat audibly and returned his hands to the steering wheel. He turned his head toward the windshield and watched the blinds of the trailers on each side of the row flip shut as his eyes turned toward them.

"Well, then I'd say I might have to ask why Emily's got blue snot dripping out of her nose and why Walter is higher than a kite. I might even have to call your good friends over there at the child protective services office and see if they might want to know about both of your present conditions now that your kids are in care," Terry said.

He turned his head back to Emily and Walter.

Emily was working herself up. She had tears welling up in her glassy eyes, and the blue snot was flowing from her nose, mixed with a generous portion of green now.

"You tell him, Dirty," Emily said. "You tell him right now."

Walter looked over at Emily and moved to put one of his gigantic chubby paws on her back. She saw it coming and tried to jerk away and nearly fell but caught herself on the cruiser's door.

"You tell him right now, Dirty. We don't need to

be hiding him," Emily said.

"Now, come on, Em. He's your—" Walter started.

Emily turned toward him faster than Walter or Terry expected. Her open hand lashed across his face with a smack. Terry watched the lava lamp-like motion of Walter "Dirty" Skaggs's fat face responding to the slap.

"Jesus Christ," Walter said, his words a slurred yelp. He rocked on his feet, lost his balance, and flumped back onto the steps of the crooked porch.

"I know he's my brother, damnit, but he got churched just the same. You said you talked to him yesterday. Now you tell Trooper Terry," Emily said, smearing blue and green across her face as she tried to wipe away the tears.

Walter rubbed his hand across his cheek and looked up into Terry's understanding and smiling face and told him where JJ Conn was living.

****

"Whoever did it was after Larry Whitaker, himself. There was no money taken from the register, and nothing of value appears to be missing from the Store," Det. Stewart said.

"Or for the joy of the thing," Terry added.

The case had been reassigned to Stewart, recently promoted to detective and transferred from Post 2, now that the icicles were forming.

"Are there any questions or suggestions?" Stewart asked.

None of the troopers or detectives raised their hands or spoke.

"All right, then, Sgt. Polk?" Stewart said, giving the floor back to Polk.

"You got anything you'd like to add?" Polk asked, looking at Terry just as he was sitting down.

Terry paused and recalled Katherine "Kate" Johnson's gasp and shocked face all those weeks ago at the Red Tin Cabin.

"No, sir," Terry said and sat down.

Terry turned to Stewart and said, "But if you need anything, I'd be happy to help."

Stewart smiled, and the briefing was complete. Everybody filed out of the conference room.

Stewart called to Terry as he was walking out the door.

"Yes?" Terry asked.

"I've read through the case file," Stewart said, holding a manila folder up.

Terry nodded his head and waited for the rest of it.

"You interviewed Katherine Johnson and Kevin Ballard the day after Larry Whitaker was murdered. The report said you saw them drive by the scene, tracked 'em down, and interviewed them at a rental cabin in Wolfe County," Stewart said.

"Yes?" Terry pointed at his watch, indicating it was time to get to the point.

"Katherine Johnson said she thought something bad happened to Larry Whitaker for his having talked to herself and Kevin Ballard because they saw somebody drive by in a white truck slowly, somebody that met the description of Jeremiah Jeffrey Conn," Stewart said.

"Yes, that's right, but JJ Conn's cult alibi stuck. We didn't have anything other than a couple of strangers saying they saw somebody matching Conn's description drive by and Larry Whitaker appear afraid afterward," Terry said.

Stewart nodded his head but looked puzzled.

"It all swings on circumstantial evidence, and the county attorney won't touch it if he doesn't think he can win," Terry said.

"And Katherine Johnson is still missing. How many days has it been now?" Stewart asked.

****

After the fork, the road was no longer paved. Deep ruts of sludge and runoff pockmarked the dirt and gravel drive; the weeds, brush, and trees crowded against and topped the cruiser, suffocating and close. The clouds were rolling overhead, and thunder rumbled off in the distance. Terry took note of the odometer at the fork and totaled eight miles when they pulled up to the clearing.

Behind the slate gray one-story house sat a dilapidated salmon-colored singlewide. It hadn't been there the first time Terry had come out.

The white truck wasn't there.

"He ain't here," Terry said.

He pulled the car up to the house and opened the door, leaving the engine running. Terry walked up the steps and knocked on the door. From what he could tell, from the window beside the front door, the house was dark inside, but Terry expected this, there were no power lines out this far. Conn probably had a generator somewhere around.

Stewart walked over to the side of the house, and Terry watched as he peered into a window.

Terry knocked again, stepped off to the side, in case it were to fly open, and listened for any sounds within. He didn't hear any.

Terry walked around the house, then circled the rundown trailer. There was a padlock on the front door, and every window was covered, the living room by a tattered confederate flag, the rest by cardboard and faded newspaper. He knocked on the door and listened.

"Come on, Stewart," Terry said. "He ain't here."

Stewart took a last look in the window of the gray house and walked back across the dirt and gravel clearing. Terry and Stewart shut their doors as the first raindrops began to fall.

****

She heard a vehicle pull up near the trailer. She heard two doors slam shut. Kate held her breath and tried to control her shaking.

Was this the reason she was being held? Were these people coming to get her?

She heard several faint knocks and the sound of men's voices. As they were knocking on the door of the gray house, her mind raced. *He must not be with them. They would know she was in the trailer if he was with them or told them.*

She fought the urge to scream out for help.

Who else would have business with the man but other men like him?

Although she was dirty, hungry, and nearly naked, she hadn't been beaten or raped.

Who knows who these people were or what they were capable of?

Kate pulled her knees up to her chest and rested her chin on them and kept quiet, stealing breaths through the clenched teeth of her chattering jaw.

****

The day after Larry Whitaker was killed, Terry had

tracked down Katherine Johnson and Kevin Ballard to the Red Tin Cabin, a rental cabin, not far from the Store in Wolfe County. He had knocked on the door, and they had let him in. He told them about seeing them drive by, and they didn't deny it. Good start.

Terry asked them about Whitaker, and they didn't deny talking to him. Even better.

Terry asked them about the nature of their business with Whitaker, and the woman, Katherine Johnson, jumped a couple of hoops ahead and knew something awful must have happened to him. She was the smarter of the two, in Terry's opinion, even if she didn't have a D and R in front of her name.

Katherine Johnson said she and Dr. Ballard had been out at the Store the day before for gas and got to talking with Mr. Whitaker. Ms. Johnson said she asked Larry Whitaker what he knew about a plant they were studying in the Gorge, this white-haired goldenrod they say can only be found here in the Gorge.

That's when Dr. Ballard joined in, talking about the plants. Dr. Ballard said they were out on a research grant regarding the plant. Dr. Ballard said he and Ms. Johnson—he called her Kate—found whole hordes of the plant with their leaves cut off. Ballard expressed his outrage at the conscious butchering of a threatened species. Ballard said he thinks the culprit had probably done enough damage to shift the plant from being merely threatened to being a full-on endangered species.

What Ballard probably thought was a moment of silence for the weeds followed that, but Terry wasn't concerned about any plants. Terry was watching both Ms. Johnson and Dr. Ballard, weighing their words, looking for a tic, a hint of fabrication or deceit. Terry had known Larry Whitaker for quite some time now, having lived in Wolfe County for the past several months. Hell, he even busted him for fighting cocks in the not so distant past. Yet he hadn't met one person that expressed ill will toward the man, even the pair that lost a lot of money and put in the tip had nothing but nice things to say.

Ms. Johnson brought that sidebar around full circle. She said she had asked Larry Whitaker about the plant and said he had told them some peculiar things that neither one of them had heard of before. She said Mr. Whitaker had told them that Native Americans had somehow created the plant, but he didn't tell them how.

Ballard said he could've been talking about the Native Americans engineering a new species of goldenrod for religious purposes through crossbreeding and seemed in awe of the idea.

Ms. Johnson said Mr. Whitaker told them that some folks in the area used to use the thin leaves to uncover hidden meanings from Bible verses. Ms. Johnson said Mr. Whitaker made it out that some folks still did.

Ballard said the old man got spooked when a white pickup drove by slowly and threw them out, so he could take a nap. Spooked, like some half-feral cat seeing a man come around the corner.

Terry listened to the description of the man in the white pickup and knew who it was right away, despite never having met the man personally. Jeremiah Jeffrey Conn was well-known in these parts. He seemed larger than life from the stories Terry had heard; he was well past Terry's own six feet and not a lick of it was fat either.

Conn had been something of a religious prodigy from all accounts. His mother took him to one of the smaller, one-room Holiness churches up Black Creek. Said he spoke in tongues before he learned how to talk.

Don't all babies babble? he thought.

People said he was "anointed by God" and was spitting sermons by twelve. They say he "perished in the Spirit" around that time, too, languishing on the floorboard, penanced for his sins at twelve years old. He traveled with tent revivals throughout the south in his teenage years.

Terry could hear his grandfather say, "Ordained and trained by God Almighty." Even his mother would nod her approval when Grandpa said that. See, at the heart of his grandfather's and mother's theological differences was the grace, or the gracelessness, of evangelism. Grandpa saw evangelizing as stepping on God's toes; God chose who He chose, and who are you to alter this? When his mother wasn't around, Grandpa would go further and call her brand the *talley takers*, saying they should be spending more time on getting right with God than tallying how many people were at their services.

After talking with Ballard and Kate Johnson, Terry paid Conn's sister, Emily and her boyfriend, a man everyone referred to simply as "Dirty," a visit and got them to talk.

Terry found JJ Conn at his little gray house, some eight miles up a narrow, winding path Terry refused to think of as a road.

If JJ Conn was surprised by Terry's visit, he didn't show it. Conn just smiled. He had a way of smiling that made the hair on the back of your neck stand up. Terry had heard people say it before, saying it was due "to the closeness of God in him." Terry didn't hold this assumption.

"Morning, JJ," Terry said.

"Morning, Trooper?" Conn said, taking a step closer to read Terry's name badge. "Terry. Morning, Trooper Terry."

Terry opened his mouth to correct him, but Conn beat him to it.

"Say, aren't you kin to one of Kennith Conn's boys? A grandson by marriage or some such? From over in Red Lick way?"

Terry did not want to get into a discussion about his relatives, however distant, with the man.

"JJ, I came out here to talk to you about something else," Terry said.

Conn looked down at Terry and leaned in a little closer, his foul breath warm on Terry's forehead and cheeks.

"What about then?" Conn asked, smiling.

Conn didn't ask Terry inside. Instead he stepped out, closed the door, then leaned back against it, his head nearly touching the top of the doorframe.

Terry took a step back and adjusted his belt; he felt the butt of his pistol, and it comforted him.

"About Tuesday, JJ. What did you do this past Tuesday?" Terry asked, paying close attention to the man's face and hands, alternately.

Conn crossed his arms across his chest. He looked over Terry to the cruiser, then off into the woods beyond.

"Tuesday, we had a meetin' up Sand Lick Fork,"

Conn said.

"Sand Lick Fork's a-ways from here. Who all was with you?" Terry asked, pulling his notepad from his pocket and clicking the pen.

Conn smiled down at Det. Terry, whose hands suddenly felt too occupied with the pen and pad.

"Wait a minute. I think I remember seeing in the register a while back about your little girl getting 'baptized' over at the Church of God. Abigail's her name, ain't it?"

Terry felt his skin crawl. He'd told Francine it wasn't a good idea to go and put that in the paper, but he'd lost that argument, like most arguments they had. Francine got saved after their divorce was finalized and had Abi baptized in the small pool they had in the church house. Francine said the other members of the church had taken out a small place in the church paper, which circulated around Wolfe County, and had to do the same for herself and for Abi. Terry didn't approve but didn't force the issue for Abi's sake.

"I'm not here on any family business of my own," Terry said. "Who all else was with you up Sand Lick?"

Conn nodded his head and gave Terry a list of six names, recalling each of their phone numbers and addresses from memory.

Terry scribbled it all down and returned the notepad to his pocket, finding it a relief to have his hands free.

"I'll be seeing you around, JJ," Terry said, opening the car door.

"I'm sure you will be, Trooper Terry."

Conn smiled.

"Trooper Terry," he called as Terry shut his door.

Terry rolled down the window and looked up at Conn.

"They can call it whatever they want over there in that high-falutin' excuse for a church, but it ain't a *real* baptism unless it's in the living water like the Lord Jesus had in the River Jordan," Conn said. "You want that little girl of yours truly saved, you bring her to me anytime, and I'll cleanse her soul with the coolness of the running water of the Almighty."

Conn twisted open the door with long, bone white fingers and disappeared into the darkness of the gray house.

****

Terry checked each of the six names after leaving JJ Conn's place, and each one checked out. JJ had a solid alibi for nearly the entire day and night of Larry Whitaker's murder, dunking babies and adults the same in the South Fork Red River and the Sand Lick Fork, then sermonizing the public on a wide array of topics, from the dangers of outside intrusion into near at hand problems, great Satan's power of temptation, salvation through prayer and God's intervention and so on.

Terry spoke with each of the six, and their stories were all the same, each differing only on what parts of the sermon they liked best. Terry didn't believe them, but they'd hold up in a court of law.

Chapter Ten

Terry thought he had stumbled onto the big break. He thought Ballard was going to chitter like a songbird now that he had his cage rattled. Terry wasn't expecting Ballard's great divulgence to be withholding evidence. Ballard had no clue where Katherine Johnson was. Ballard agreed to the polygraph against the advice of Ronald Wright, and Terry ran the gamut on him.

"Dr. Ballard, do you know where Katherine Johnson is?" Terry asked.

"No, I don't," Ballard said.

"Did you have any direct involvement in her disappearance?"

"No," Ballard said, shaking his head vehemently.

"Did you have any involvement in any way in her disappearance that you know of?"

"Not that I know of. I love her, goddamnit. I wouldn't let anything happen to her if I could help it."

There were tears in his eyes, and they spilt out onto his cheeks, but he held his composure; he didn't blubber, at least.

"Did you ever hurt Katherine Johnson, either on purpose or accident?"

"No. Never."

It appeared Ballard was telling the truth. Terry turned and looked into the one-way mirror at himself briefly. He knew Polk was going to throw a shitfit, but he had to know.

"Did you kill Angela Rogers?" Terry asked. He swore he could almost hear the scuttling of chairs from behind the glass.

"No. Absolutely not. I found her like that."

"What about your mother? Did you kill Evelyn Ballard?"

"No. Jesus Christ. No, I would never."

"Did you kill Larry Whitaker?"

"No. No, I did not kill anybody," Ballard yelled, leaping to his feet.

The door behind Ballard burst open, and Polk barged into the room.

"Get your ass out here, Terry," Polk said.

Polk's face was redder than most tomatoes Terry had ever recalled seeing.

****

"You know better," Sgt. Polk said.

He'd walked Ballard back to his office and spoke with him behind the closed door for nearly fifteen minutes. Tones of a reserved placation. Then the door opened up, and Polk walked Ballard and his flustered attorney to the waiting room.

Polk took Terry by the arm and walked him into his office. He slammed the door shut.

"What in God's name were you thinking?"

"I had to know, sir," Terry said.

"You *had* to know? You know very damn well that you just compromised those other investigations. You could've had your chance to get those answers without overstepping your bounds and taking a shit all over another detective's investigation," Polk said.

He was mad, the veins in his neck stood out and

another throbbed on his left temple, just under his graying hair. Polk hardly ever cursed after he made sergeant. He'd found Jesus about the same time and was baptized in the same mini-swimming pool that Francine and Abi were. Terry pictured his grandfather leaning in and saying confidentially, *If the Lord didn't call you, don't come a running. People all the time tripping over themselves trying to do somebody else's job.*

Ballard didn't do it. The polygraph assisted Terry with coming to grips with that. He felt he could live with whatever storm blew through the bureaucratic tail winds. Polk was still yelling, but the shade of red had paled, nearly back to his normal pink.

"You better hope your ass Post 4 doesn't take this to the commissioner, Terry." Polk pointed to the door, signifying the end of the conversation.

****

A trooper followed Kevin back to the cabin and took his mother's copy of *Nolin & the Hellbenders* into evidence. He felt so stupid for keeping it but better now that he'd told Det. Terry. Kevin felt Terry had had it in for him this whole time and was happy to clear the air with the polygraph, against Ron Wright's vocal objections. He told him that polygraphs could give false readings and weren't admissible in court in most cases, but the results could still ruin Kevin and his career.

He took it anyway. Kevin wanted Kate back, and he didn't know how else to help. He took the test in hopes that the energy, however slight, that was used in harboring doubts about his involvement in her disappearance would now be spent on finding her.

Kevin didn't know whether to stay at the Red Tin

or head back to Lexington. He called Dr. Clark, the department head, that next morning. He'd spoken with him a few days after Kate disappeared and had promised to call back with more information when he had it. At that time, Dr. Clark had put the study on hold and Kevin didn't argue. He couldn't have focused on it then.

During this phone call, Kevin told Dr. Clark that he wanted to pick the reins back up and continue the research while the police looked for Kate. Kevin said he needed to be doing something other than sitting and waiting by the phone. Dr. Clark refused initially, but Kevin worked him over. There was research to do. Kevin was qualified to do it and needed to get back into his routine. He felt like a fish out of water. Plus, the research grant had to be used completely, or it wouldn't be offered to the department next year. Dr. Clark agreed on the condition that Kevin take on an assistant: Kinders.

Kinders had returned to Lexington that Friday after Kevin took the polygraph. Kevin thanked him for his help and for being there. Kevin told him he was glad he had a friend he knew he could count on and—in typical Kinders fashion—Kinders told Kevin to save his "big, fat, wet kisses" for when the police found Kate.

Dr. Clark arranged for Kinders' intro biology classes and labs to be covered by another assistant professor, and Kinders returned to the Red Tin Cabin later Monday afternoon, only hours after Kevin had spoken with the department head.

There had been a knock at the door, that Kevin now kept locked. Then, in came Kinders, bearing a backpack of clothes and an air mattress.

"That couch doesn't sleep worth a shit," Kinders said, dropping the air mattress on the living room floor. "Dr. Clark said he wanted me to help you count flowers, and I figured, what the hell. It's better than explaining photosynthesis to a bunch of overprivileged fraternity morons."

His words had none of the bite they'd had before Kate disappeared. Kevin got the sense Kinders did indeed have a heart somewhere in there and was doing his best to lighten things up.

"Thanks for helping out," Kevin said. "Are you familiar with *Solidago albopilosa*?"

"What do you think?" Kinders replied.

"Didn't think so. Ok, let's go over it. It'll be easier telling you here than on the trail," Kevin said, sitting down at the table.

Kinders pulled out a chair and joined him.

****

The fog hung loosely around the Red Tin Cabin like a patchy quilt, spilling stuffing. Kevin and Kinders set out before daybreak. They took Kevin's SUV to the Osborne Bend trailhead. Kevin slid the backpack around his arms and shut the hatch.

"You ready?" Kevin asked.

Kinders looked half-asleep.

"Yeah," Kinders said, shutting the passenger side door and following Kevin across the parking lot.

The morning was cool and crisp, their breath smoking out of their mouths, dissipating before their eyes. Kevin shivered under the thin long jacket but knew he'd warm up on the trail. Once the sun got up and going, he wouldn't even need it.

"Jesus Christ," Kinders said.

Kevin turned around and saw that Kinders was looking at the trail map.

"Seven miles?"

An impish smile momentarily flickered on Kevin's face, but then his stomach sank. The trail seemed incomplete without Kate's euphonious mirth, a blossoming spring morning without the twittering peter-peter-peter calls of the tufted titmouse. Kevin turned back to the trail and headed on.

The two men walked in silence for some time. The morning sun peeked over the ridge, sunshine filtering through branches in long, luminous shafts. They passed seven sedentary white-tailed deer standing still as statues; their heads followed the men as they passed but never seemed to actually move.

When he and Kate started this study, it had been a relief to leave their cell phones in the car or at the Red Tin. They were getting away from their electronic lives, ignoring emails, text messages, social networking.

As he walked some ten paces ahead of Kinders, Kevin couldn't help but wish his cell phone, which was in his front pocket, would ring, so he could fill his ears with Kate's melodious laughter.

****

"Castle Goldenrod," Kinders announced as they approached the rockhouse.

Ballard held the chicken wire down for Kinders to step over.

"Lower thy bridge so that I may cross thine moat, sire," Kinders said, taking a small bow before stepping over the wire.

Kinders made a trumpeting noise, then held down the fence for Ballard.

"Your king, minions," he called out.

They walked farther in. Ballard took off the backpack and pulled out the notebook and the camera.

"You want to count 'em up or document any damage?" Ballard asked.

"I'm all rock and roll, baby," Kinders said, taking the camera from Ballard's hands.

"All we need is directly around the plants and something like a twenty-yard radius around the abri," Ballard said, dropping to his knees in front of "Occurrence 34" as this cluster of plants was labeled in the notebook.

"The what?"

"Rock shelter," Ballard said, not bothering to look up.

Kinders watched him for a minute. Ballard slid his fingers deliberately and softly about the grouping of plants. Kinders could tell Ballard wasn't himself, but he hadn't seen any signs that Ballard was really losing it, and his professionalism hadn't sloshed off a bit. Sure, he'd heard him up there in the loft crying, but who wouldn't? Kinders didn't know how he'd react in Ballard's position and came to the conclusion that Ballard was something of a saint.

Ballard had even expressed genuine concern over the welfare of the weed they were studying. When Ballard was briefing him about finding so many of them hacked, Kinders thought the man might have gotten a little misty even.

"Goddamnit," Ballard said. "Somebody cut these, too. The fuckers. Gonna have to talk to the rangers."

Kinders wondered if Ballard had cared this much about the plants before Kate disappeared. *Yeah, I bet he did. I bet he acted just like that when he found 'em all cut up, too.*

Despite his qualifications and employment, Kinders found it impossible to actually care about these puny, little goldenrods and was baffled that Ballard could. *Sanctity often requires the focus of time for clarification,* he mused.

Kinders photographed the area around the cluster and the chicken wire fencing blocking off both entrances to the rockhouse. Kinders stepped over the fence on the far side of the rockhouse and took a few pictures of a crushed Mountain Dew can, an empty cigarette pack, and a candy bar wrapper. Somebody had stopped for a snack before hiking on. Kinders didn't see any trash on the inside of the enclosure and guessed the hikers just wanted a somewhat level place to rest.

Kinders followed the ledge down into the forest, scanning the mountain side for trash, old campfires, and the like. He cut-stepped through a patch of young sour gum trees and gasped.

A gigantic, pale man was taking a shit. The man's back was to Kinders, and he didn't show any sign that he had heard Kinders' approach or his comical gasp at the disgusting sight he'd stumbled onto. The man dropped a tremendously large section of fecal matter. Kinders felt sick. As he turned to go back the way he had come, the man spoke. "All is within the sight of the Almighty." The man's voice was quiet and something akin to serene.

Kinders turned back and saw that the man had pulled his jeans back up and was buttoning them, staring at Kinders.

"I'm sorry, I didn't—"

The man's eyes bore into Kinders, who broke the contact, and his eyes darted down to the pile near the large man's clown-like feet. Kinders noted the absence of toilet paper.

"For His eyes are upon the ways of man, and He seeth all his goings. There is no darkness, nor shadow of death, where the workers of iniquity may hide themselves," the man said.

Kinders felt a trickle of ice water drip down his spine.

The man turned and walked down into the forest. There was no trail for him to follow, but he appeared to know exactly where he was going. Kinders lifted the camera and snapped several shots of the man disappearing into the wilderness.

****

"Cool if I rest my eyes while you run in?" Kinders asked.

"Yeah. Shouldn't take more than ten minutes."

Kevin pulled into the parking lot, left the engine running with Kinders in the passenger seat, and went into the ranger's station. The windows were fogged over, and a fan sluggishly moved the steam heat around the room.

"Good morning," an energetic man said from behind the counter.

"Morning," Kevin said.

"What can I do for you?"

"I'm Dr. Kevin Ballard with the University of Kentucky. I'm researching—"

"The white-haired goldenrod," the ranger finished.

Kevin nodded his head and gave the man a wan smile. "That's right. I've got some concerns that I think

I need to address with you all," Kevin said. "I've been to a little over half of the documented occurrences thus far and found the plants heavily damaged and dying. Somebody's been cutting the leaves off."

"We put up the chicken wire and the signs," the ranger began.

"Yes, and I think that's stopped your average hiker from damaging the plants, but whoever is taking the leaves hasn't been deterred."

Kevin turned the camera on and opened up several pictures of the cut plants and showed them to the ranger. Kevin read the nametag on the man's shirt as he looked at the pictures: Jim Bower. Ranger Bower's face wrinkled as he scrolled through the pictures.

"I've heard that some people call it 'White-Sight' and use it in some sort of religious practice. Do you know anything about all of that?" Kevin asked.

The ranger nodded his head slowly and rubbed his chin.

"Yessir, I do," Ranger Bower said. "There used to be quite a number of folks that believed in it. Called it 'leaf reading.' I never held no confidence in it, but to each their own, I guess," Ranger Bower said.

Kevin nodded his understanding.

"My daddy used to run around with some of them leaf readers, though he was born and raised Springwell Holiness. He got some sidelong looks on Sundays 'cause of that." Ranger Bower smiled. "Used to embarrass the hell out of my mother."

"There was something about the Native Americans," Kevin said, hoping to steer Ranger Bower clear of more personal reverie.

"Ah, yes. They used to say that angels had

144

bestowed foresight onto the Indians that were here before the place was settled, if you could ever call it that. Folks said the Indians knew the white folks were coming and that the white folks had work to do to get ready for Jesus's return. So they became the White-Sight, the foreseeing leaves the white man used to read the good Lord's instructions," Ranger Bower said.

Kevin's eyebrows shot up, and his head dipped forward, shaking, toward the ranger.

"What you're telling me is that the Native Americans sacrificed themselves to white settlers to bring about the return of Jesus Christ?" Kevin asked.

"Listen, now. You asked about the leaf readers, and I told you." Ranger Bower stiffened.

Kevin kept shaking his head in disbelief. "Do people still believe any of that?"

"Well, I'm not sure about that, Dr. Ballard," Ranger Bower said. "Haven't met a one, but you hear rumors from time to time, especially from the ones that have a tighter grip on their Bibles than most."

"*Solidago albopilosa* is a *federally* protected plant. It might be an endangered species because of the damage of these 'leaf readers.' What're you doing to stop them?"

"We've been putting up chicken wire and the signs."

"The chicken wire and signs aren't stopping these wingnuts from killing the plants."

"The budget—" Ranger Bower began.

"Jesus Christ," Kevin said.

****

Kevin slammed the door shut, startling Kinders awake.

"Shit, man. What's the problem?"

Kevin threw it in reverse and peeled out of the parking lot.

"We're not going to be getting any help from Ranger Dingus," Kevin said. "Hand me my phone. I'm gonna call Detective Terry, see if he can come out this afternoon and take a look at those pictures you took yesterday. Maybe one of the goddamn authorities will start providing some assistance."

****

"He was taking a shit right there in the woods," Kinders said, shaking his head. "And he didn't wipe as far as I could tell."

Det. Terry looked up from the camera and turned to Kevin. "So you want me to be on the lookout for somebody with a shitty ass?"

"This looks like the freak show in the white truck we saw driving by the Store," Kevin said. "Repeat what he said to Det. Terry for me, Kinders. Listen, now, and tell me this doesn't like somebody crazy enough to kill for the insanity they keep."

"Something along the lines of 'God sees all, the workers of iniquity will have nowhere to hide.' I looked up what I remembered of it, and I'm about 99 percent sure he quoted straight from the Book of Job," Kinders said.

Kinders pulled his phone out, found the search screen, and read from the Book of Job, chapter thirty-four, verses twenty-one and twenty-two, "'For His eyes are upon the ways of men, and He seeth all his goings. There is no darkness, nor shadow of death, where the workers of iniquity may hide themselves.' I distinctly remember that huge bastard using the word *iniquity* and

146

saying that the workers of iniquity had nowhere to hide."

"So you're both 'workers of iniquity'?" Det. Terry asked.

"In the eyes of a nutbag, I very well could be. So could Kinders. So could Kate. I can't tell you how many times I've read or heard fundamentalists say that evolution was nothing more than demonic propaganda from Great Satan himself. My mother was murdered, and the message was left for me, I'm sure of it. *Hellbenders* pretty much sealed the deal. I think some sicko is trying to hurt me for what they must see as peddling the Devil's gospel," Kevin said, stopping to take a breath. "I know it may sound incredibly narcissistic, but I don't think it is. You have to look at the thing from their eyes."

"I'll look into it," Det. Terry said, after scribbling the last words into his notepad and returning it to his breast pocket.

Kevin looked away. "Goddamnit. Is this person going to have to gut me and string me up on a cross in front of the courthouse for you all to do anything about it? That freak has Kate, and there's no telling what horrors she's experiencing."

****

Terry knew it was JJ Conn that Jason Kinders ran across off the beaten path. That's always where a man like JJ Conn lurked: off the beaten path. He made his home a hop, skip, and jump on outward, past the outskirts of civilized behavior and rationalized thinking. This warranted the snake slinging and fire handling, the yodeling in unintelligible gibberish.

It didn't provide for kidnapping and murder

though.

It couldn't, could it?

Terry pulled back onto Natural Bridge Road and headed back to Thomason's Trailer Court for another little talk with Emily and Dirty.

****

The search teams grew smaller and smaller with each passing day without any progress. In six days' time, no one knocked on the Red Tin Cabin's door to start the search in the morning, and the great communions of artificial light no longer convened each night.

Katherine Johnson had been set aside as a brief at the end of the news roundup: *Still missing*.

****

Kinders and Kevin had been at it hard the past two days. Miles and miles of trails and dozens of occurrences of *Solidago albopilosa*. The two men did not talk much, but Kevin was glad to have Kinders there. Kinders gave him an excuse to swallow all those insecure feelings of loss, hurt, fear. The shame at being helpless, useless. Having Kinders on the trail kept Kevin focused and professional.

Having Kinders at the Red Tin kept Kevin from losing it. He couldn't help the tears that came upon waking in the night and expecting Kate to be there and finding that she wasn't. But these weren't hysterics. It was a deeper hurt, and he cringed and held his breath until it passed. Then he slept, exhausted, again.

Kevin had tracked and documented nearly half of all reported occurrences: fifty-three clusters and nearly twenty-thousand individual white-haired goldenrods. Kevin felt a slight sense of accomplishment that disappeared as soon as he acknowledged it.

They had just concluded their morning work and had sat down to lunch in the rockhouse when Kevin's phone rang. He dropped his sandwich and slid the phone out of his pocket. He recognized the area code, 270, to be from central and western Kentucky, but he didn't know the number.

"Hello?" Kevin said.

"Mr. Ballard? Oh, I'm sorry. Dr. Ballard?" an elderly man's voice asked.

"Yes, this is Dr. Kevin Ballard. Who am I speaking with?"

"This is Emmanuel Stephens. Your mother's, God rest her soul, attorney."

Kevin slapped his hand against his forehead and groaned. "Mr. Stephens, I am so sorry. I forgot all about our appointment. A lot has happened since last week."

"I'm sorry to hear about Ms. Johnson, Dr. Ballard. Your aunt told me about that situation. I've put off calling you about your mother's will, but I fear I'll be traveling soon and don't know when I'll be able to reschedule our appointment if we can't squeeze one in before next Friday."

"I apologize again, Mr. Stephens. Is there any way we could complete this over the phone?" Kevin asked. He picked his sandwich back up and brushed the sandy grit off it.

"No, Dr. Ballard, I'm afraid not. Your mother was very specific in the will that I must personally see to it. Could we schedule it for next Thursday?" Mr. Stephens paused, and Kevin heard the rustling of papers. He continued, "The seventh of May?"

"Ok, that's fine. See you then. Thanks. Bye,"

Kevin said and ended the call.

"What was all that about?" Kinders asked through a mouthful of cheese-flavored chips.

"My mother's will. I have to go back to Hardin County next week to meet with her attorney about it."

"When?" Kinders asked.

"Next Thursday."

Kevin bit into the sandwich; he felt the grit of the sandy soil but tasted the bologna.

"I guess that means I'll get a nice long weekend, free of chicken wire motes and white-haired castles. Yippee," Kinders said.

Kevin finished his sandwich in silence and put the garbage in his backpack.

****

They hiked out to three more occurrences in the area that afternoon and made it back to the vehicle just before the sun sank behind the mountains. They were both sweat-drenched and hungry. The drive back to the Red Tin Cabin passed by in a blur of dark blue branches waving and the howling of the wind through the open windows.

Kevin turned off onto the drive and crossed the creek. He looked over and saw that Kinders had fallen asleep. He reached over and jabbed Kinders on the triceps. Kinders mumbled something that Kevin didn't understand but didn't wake up.

They topped the ridge and the headlights fell on the Red Tin Cabin's open door. All the lights were off, including the front floodlights that Kevin had turned on when they left earlier that morning. Kevin put the car in park but left the engine running and the headlights trained on the open front door.

Kevin slid his phone out of his pocket. It had less than two percent battery left.

"Of course," Kevin said and let the phone drop into the cup holder.

"Kinders, wake up."

Kinders sat up in the seat and rubbed his eyes. "Sorry, Ballard. Those trails. I'm beat," Kinders said and clicked off his seat belt.

"Look."

Kinders followed Kevin's pointing finger out the windshield, through the high beams of the headlights to the tall, pale man standing in the open door of the Red Tin Cabin.

"Jesus Christ," Kinders hissed. "It's him."

Chapter Eleven

Terry pulled the cruiser up to the trailer and laid on
the horn. The sun was beginning its slow descent
behind the hills to the west. Terry had the windows
down and listened but didn't hear anything.

Terry cut the engine and got out the car. He took
the steps all at once and banged on the door with the
side of his hand, hard.

"Emily," Terry yelled. "Open up. It's Detective
Terry."

Nothing from inside the trailer.

"Walter, are you in there? Open the goddamn
door."

He turned to the trailers around him. Blinds moved
and heads ducked.

Terry tried the knob and the door opened. He
pushed it in, and it groaned to a stop about halfway
open. He removed his Smith & Wesson 1076 from the
holster but kept the safety on.

"Police. This is the Kentucky State Police," Terry
called.

There was no answer.

Terry stepped into the doorframe and tried the light
switch, but nothing happened. He flipped the safety off
and stepped into the trailer.

****

Emily Conn and Walter "Dirty" Skaggs must've

left in a hurry. In front of the soiled and sunken couch, on the coffee table, was a small white plate. On the white plate was an inch and a half line of crushed blue powder and a rolled up one-dollar bill. There were no signs of any violence from what Terry could tell in the mess of the place. He checked each of the rooms of the trailer, but he didn't find anything or anybody.

Terry stepped out onto the porch and pulled the door to. He stepped off the porch and opened the door of the car, but a voice called out, "Hey."

A thin woman stood barefoot beside the next trailer, down on the left. She motioned for Terry to come over. Terry shut the door and crossed the gravel and the dirt to where the woman stood on a small patch of dead grass.

"They ain't here," the woman said.

She looked between thirty and forty years old, but it was always hard to tell when drugs were involved.

"No shit," Terry said.

"They up'n left with that tall one."

Terry appraised this woman more closely. She was definitely high; her eyes were glassy, her voice distant, the words slurred, and she rocked on her bare feet. She had a little red dot on the fold of her left arm, the "ditch" they called it, and a little moisture moved slowly down her forearm, where he could see the pressure marks from whatever she had used to tie off. The more he looked at her, the more he wished he had gotten into the car and gone on home.

"Ma'am, you realize I am an officer of the law, don't you? You need to decide real quick whether you have any information that I would find pertinent or get your ass back in that trailer before you catch a PI."

"Now, I'm not concerned with your law, only the law of the Almighty. But I do fear for 'em. There's stories going 'round 'bout that big 'un. And they just got them kids taken, and they're trying by God, through God, to get 'em back, and I'm afraid that tall one, he's gonna drag them into something deeper than they can swim out of," the woman's shaky voice broke, and she rocked from foot to foot.

"Are you talking about JJ Conn?" Terry asked her, bringing out the notepad and pen.

"Yessir. Everybody 'round here knows about him. Been preaching since he was kid. He's been going 'round the county telling people they's wrong and he's got the right." The woman shook her head like she was trying to clear it. "Say he's a leaf reader and all that though." She waved her hand. She leaned in confidentially, "You know he got churched for what he did to that Macon boy, don't ye?"

"What in God's name are you talking about?"

"You ain't from here, are ye?"

Terry flipped the notepad shut and returned it, along with the pen, to his breast pocket. He removed the handcuffs from his belt and raised them up until they were directly in front of the woman's face.

"You're going to jail in five seconds flat, unless you tell me where Emily and Dirty went with JJ Conn," Terry said.

The woman jerked her head back on her shoulders, as if she smelled something pungent. She began to get all worked up like they do. "Now, wait a minute. I's just trying to help. You don't have no reason to throw me in jail."

"Did he make them go with him, or did they go of

154

their own free will?"

"The big one, he pulled up in that white truck and blew the horn. Em came out and told him she didn't want no dealings with him, that he'd been churched, and he knew how she felt about that. The big one just sat in the truck and smiled at her. I couldn't tell what he said because his voice was so quiet, but he was saying something. Something Em didn't like. She started crying, saying no, that she'd call the law and how could he do that." The woman steadied the more she spoke.

Terry didn't interrupt her. He removed the notepad again and jotted down his shorthand of what she told him.

"That big one he said something else and Em turned 'round real fast and went back in the trailer. I couldn't hear what they were saying, but they were in there screeching like two cats. They both came out with shoes and jackets and got in that white truck with him, and he pulled on out and they left. Couple of hours ago now, not real sure on the time."

Terry nodded his head and finished scribbling. "What's your name, darlin'?" he asked.

"Sheila Hamilton."

Terry wrote it down with the rest of her information and got back in the car. As he started the engine, he got a call of a domestic up Black Creek. An Emily Conn had called in saying her brother was threatening their parents, her boyfriend, and herself.

Terry pulled out of the trailer court, flipped on his lights, and sped toward Black Creek.

****

The whole of Black Creek Branch was out and more. Terry flashed the lights and honked the horn at all the people in the narrow road. Terry had been up this way a few times before when he was still on patrol but wasn't certain which of the trailers was the Conn family's. He found out quickly that he didn't really have to; he just followed the commotion on up the mountain.

The road was barely paved for the first tenth of a mile, then reverted to gravel, and finally became a mix of gravel and dirt. Even if the roads were clear, he couldn't have done much more than ten without losing a crown.

"Jesus Christ," Terry said.

He'd never seen so many people out in a hollow like this. It looked like they were filing on up the mountain for the county fair or some great tent revival or healing crusade. He passed old men, young children, and women among the lanky, tattooed men.

"What in the blue hell is going on?"

He radioed for backup.

Terry rolled the windows up and parked the car where it was in the road. He popped the trunk and got out. He grabbed the shotgun and pocketed some shells.

The crowd watched Terry silently and parted for him as he made his way up the hill to the white trailer. He could hear them inside. The door was open, and he could hear Emily Conn crying. She was pleading; he could tell by her tone, but he couldn't make out a single word.

As Terry reached the steps, JJ Conn stepped out onto the raised porch. His eyes were alight, and he smiled, his teeth yellowed and shiny. Conn raised his hands over his head but not in surrender to Terry. He was saluting the crowd.

Terry realized the people were closing in around the trailer, their heads lifted up and their eyes on JJ Conn. Terry looked from face to face and saw nothing short of awe and adulation. Terry took one step up the porch, and a hand from behind pulled him back, and another took the shotgun. Then he was swept over, inundated by more arms than he could count or keep track of.

****

They held Terry from behind while someone removed the handcuffs from his belt and fastened them tightly around his wrists. The metal cut into his skin. They stood Terry up below the porch.

Conn smiled down on Terry. He held a black, worn leather-bound Bible with a blood red cross on the front cover in his right hand, and his left was raised level with his chest, palm out.

"Brothers and sisters, God has spoken to me and sent me to you to bear witness," Conn said. "I have been baptized in the fire. I have held the great serpents, imbibed the poisons. I have healed the sick, and I have read through the leaves." The cadence danced like a pull chain engine fighting to start; the chain was pulled, and it turned over, then settled back down. The chain was pulled again, and it roared to life, then settled back down but not completely off, just humming complacently, a power idling.

It was in this way that Conn told the crowd and Detective David Terry what God had told him.

"The Lord came to me and He told me, 'Let Me define schism for you, Jeremiah.' He said, 'Schism is a necessary step along the road to Salvation.' I believe He was telling me that I was destined, supposed to be *churched,* so that I could stand here before you now with one hand on the Good Book and the other turned up to Heaven and spread the News." Conn slapped the leather-bound Bible with his palm, the red cross blinking away with each slap.

A chorus of *amens* rippled through the crowd.

"The Good Lord, He came to me in a dream. I was laying there in my bed up in Hayfire Creek, awake. Then He sent me into a dream, and I was truly Awakened," Conn said.

Amens and a few shouts of "tell it now."

"He lifted me out of that bed, and I walked in the whiteness of Heaven hand-in-hand with our Lord, Jesus. He took me up and held my hand, I say. He told me that Heaven wasn't for everyone. Jesus told me that some people weren't going to be spending Eternity behind the pearly gates." Conn shook his head, but the smile remained intact.

"Some people, some of you here with us tonight, are going to be cast aside and fall below into the flames for the Devil to keep. Your sins shackle you to this *material* plane, and your soul will rot along with all living, *material* things. Now the older of you'ns may recollect a few that used to 'leaf read,'" Conn said, nodding his head and looking out over the crowd.

Several *yessirs* floated up to the white trailer.

"I know there's a good bunch of you'ns that ain't never heard of it 'fore now, who," JJ Conn looked down on Terry and said, "as they say, 'ain't from 'round these parts.'"

Conn smiled and there was a spattering of chuckles throughout the crowd.

"Y'all could learn something from what I'm 'bout

to tell ye." Conn paused and his eyes rolled up in his head, and he began stomping his feet on the wooden porch—slap, slap, slapslap, slap, slap, slapslap.

The crowd picked up the rhythm and clapped their hands along with him. Some slapped their thighs.

Conn continued without stopping the stomp. "He came to me in a dream and led me out of my home and into the forest, Praise Be. He took me along no marked trail but a Path of Righteousness, a Path of Light, Praise Be."

The exhortation undulated with the stomping, with the clapping, with the slapping of the thighs. Conn's quick deep breaths in between each sentence, "uh huh" they sounded, like a coda.

"He took me up in His Protective Hands, and together we walked across a great ledge on a cliff yonder, Praise Be. He didn't let me trip, and I had no fear of falling, Praise Be. He bent me down, and I bowed my head for I thought He wanted me to pray, wait now. So I looked up at the beautiful Savior from my bended knee, wait now. He told me to look at the soil under my knees, and what did I see? White-Sight from old, White-Sight from the angels that foretold, Praise Be."

Terry couldn't swallow. His mouth felt stuffed with cotton. The sweat dripped over his eyebrows and stung his eyes. The hands held him still, and he could not wipe the sweat away. The hands held his arms behind his back and used his shoulder blades to slap out the driving rhythm.

"Our Lord, Jesus Almighty, He reached down and picked one leaf off that little plant, and it did not die nor did it cause any pain. Jesus, Praise His Name. Jesus, He held this thin little leaf before me, still on bended knee I was, and He told me it would show me the things that needed doing 'fore He came back, Praise Be. He told me to hold it 'fore the Scripture and let it show what lies just behind the words, Praise Be."

From behind him, Terry could hear a mumbling. He did his best to tune out Conn. Terry heard it from more than one voice around him. He turned to his right and watched a pregnant young woman, probably in her early to mid-twenties, chanting to herself with her eyes closed. She took one step forward, then one step back, right along with the beat. Terry listened to the woman's words and realized she was not speaking English, or any other language, for that matter. The woman and several others in the crowd had slipped into some religious ecstasy and were carried away from themselves.

"Anointed I am and anointed His Chosen shall be for all time, Praise Be. We have to do what He commands, Praise Be. Resolute and strong, Praise Be. Swinging in sweet Heaven's Grace foreverlong, Praise Be," Conn sang.

Sweat dripped off his face onto the porch.

"Through the leaves He showed me, White-Sight. That there are minion devils, fallen miscreants in the darkness of idolatry who must bleed, Praise Be." Conn jumped up, then stomped onto the porch.

"I will bring the Light of the Lord to the savages."

The crowd quieted. The unintelligible language of the tongues silenced. Conn opened his black Bible with the red cross on the cover.

"'Cursed be he who does the Lord's work remissly, cursed he who holds back his sword from blood.' Book

160

of Jeremiah, chapter forty-eight, verse ten. Brothers and sisters, we got work to do." Conn closed his Bible.

"Amen."

He turned his gaze back to Terry and smiled. Conn nodded at somebody behind Terry, and an explosion of white erupted in front of his eyes, which quickly disintegrated into a darkness Terry had never before known.

Chapter Twelve

"Call the police," Kevin said.

Neither Kevin nor Kinders took their eyes off the tall, looming man staring into the bright beams of the headlights.

Kinders searched his pants pockets, then his shirt.

"Shit," Kinders said. "I left it in there."

Kevin snatched his cell from the cup holder and saw that it had died.

"Shit."

JJ Conn took a step out of the Red Tin Cabin and smiled.

"What do we do?" Kinders whispered.

Kevin shook his head.

"We should bolt."

"Kate might be in there," Kevin said.

The three men didn't move for a long moment. JJ Conn smiled toward the SUV. Kevin and Kinders sat rigid in their seats and stared out at the sallow giant. Then Kevin opened the driver's side door and stepped out into the muggy night.

****

"I have not come to call the righteous, but sinners, to repentance," JJ Conn said.

Kevin cringed at the soft but carrying voice and its words.

"What have you done?" Kevin asked.

"The Lord's work."

Kevin found nothing reassuring about the man's smile or soft voice. He felt them a thin mask, hiding the monster underneath.

"Have you repented, sinner?" JJ Conn asked.

"What have you done?" Kevin repeated, louder.

JJ Conn turned and walked back into the darkened cabin.

****

"What the fuck are you doing? Don't follow that crazy bastard," Kinders said.

Ballard left the car door open, and Kinders watched him walk woodenly across the gravel.

"Shit," Kinders said.

****

Black branches whirled across a background of Turnbull's blue. Terry's head swam in different depths of pain and muddlement. He moved his arms and felt the smooth plastic of the seat. His hands found the Easter egg on the crown of his head and he groaned. Terry hoisted himself into a sitting position and rested against the glass partition.

"You all right back there, Terry?" Stewart asked, looking through the rearview mirror from the driver's seat.

"What the fuck?" Terry said.

"What the fuck, indeed," Stewart said. "What was going on up there?"

"JJ Conn," Terry said.

His head felt twice the size it should be.

"The guy you wanted to make for Larry Whitaker?"

"The crazy bastard," Terry said.

A.S. Coomer

****

Sleeping was easier during the day when the man wasn't there. At night, he sat back there by candlelight, and it sounded like he carried on conversations with himself, one voice soft, distinct and the other an inflection, shifting tangles of syllables and consonants.

She felt a sudden uneasiness and opened her eyes to find him sitting there, cross-legged. He was already smiling at her, but he extended it noticeably at her sudden awareness.

"She wakes," he said.

Kate scrambled up off the soiled floor, into a sitting position, with her knees pulled up to her chest. She tugged at the T-shirt, trying, unsuccessfully, to cover the nakedness of her body underneath it.

"Then the eyes of both of them were opened, and they realized they were naked," the man said, his smile disappearing.

Kate shook, couldn't help it, and hated herself for the show of fear.

"You had all the fruits of the Garden of Eden, save one. One tree in the center of it all that was *not* available to you." The man rose to his feet.

He looked down at Kate and shook his head, then started pacing the length of the living room, stopping at the foot of the hall and at the end of the carpet into the kitchen.

"Try as I might, I just caint help feeling this way." He turned to her and smiled again.

It did not comfort Kate, not at all.

"He works how He works, this I know. Everything in its right place. I don't have the faculty to understand His plan. I am but a humble servant, bringing the Light

164

to those in the dark."

He dropped to his knees before her and took her shaking hands into his; his grip was ironclad, his hands as cold as ice picks.

"There's a purpose for all His creatures, you see. Each and every one. Miscreants, sodomites, and good Christians alike."

He leaned his face into Kate's, his breath obscenely hot and fetid.

"Have you ever been baptized, woman?"

****

Fear overwhelmed her. Kate couldn't force her mouth to form the words, any words.

"Have you been washed clean of your sins?" His voice dropped, barely more than a whisper, but Kate flinched. There was something so sinister in the tone.

"Y-y-yes."

The man's face receded a few inches as he settled back onto his haunches.

"Was it in the Lord's living waters?"

"What?"

She didn't understand. *Living waters? Should've said yes!* her brain screamed. *You know how these things end for those who don't go along with the program. Feign the goddamn Stockholm Syndrome if it'll help.*

But it was too late.

"The tank serves no purpose other than creating stagnant cesspools of falsehood. We will change this. Your time is soon. You, too, have a part to play."

His hands moved faster than Kate could keep track of. One second they were gripping hers; the next they weren't. Then one flashed snakelike before her eyes, and she was swimming somewhere in the void.

****

From the dark there came, at first, only flickers of light; warm, fading afternoon sunlight. Then the steady lapping, pulling at the thin T-shirt and the lank strands of her filthy hair brought her awake.

He was holding her afloat in his hard arms. She couldn't get her eyes to fully focus, her head buzzed numbly.

"Wha—"

"And Jesus replied, 'Very truly I tell you, no one can see the kingdom of God unless they are born again.' John three, three." His chin jutted toward the late afternoon sky.

Some of the fog cleared. They were in the middle of a river, the swirling water coming up to the man's chest. Thick forest surrounded them, dark foliage swaying in the breeze like a whispering, watchful congregation.

"No," she said. "No."

"God, we ask that You forgive us sinners. God, we ask that You take this particular sinner into Your flock. With this, Your flowing, living water," the man cupped a handful of water onto Kate's head, "You wash clean this fallen woman's soul."

Kate's head was jerked under. She sucked in a mouthful of the gritty water.

She sputtered as he pulled her up.

"May she see the Light of the Lord."

Just as quickly as she had come out of the current, she was dropped back in. She flailed against him, but his arms were steel cables. The silt stung her eyes and clogged her throat. He kept her under, and after an agonizing century, her struggles ceased, and all was dark once again.

****

"He's got followers. More followers than I would've imagined," Terry said, gingerly rubbing the lump on his head.

Stewart looked back at Terry through the rearview every few seconds.

"The crazy bastard," Terry said. "Where are we going?"

"Clark Regional," Stewart said. "You got a nasty whomp on your noggin. Probably a concussion, too."

Terry's head cleared momentarily, and several questions popped into his head at the same time.

"Was the girl there? Katherine Johnson?"

Stewart looked back through the rearview and said, "No. Did you see her there?"

Terry shook his head.

"Did you get Conn?"

"No, he wasn't there when I got there. Is he the one that gave you that goose egg?"

"No, he was there, though. He was standing up on that porch, sermonizing. Those people were eating it up. I don't think I've ever seen such a thing," Terry said. "What about Emily Conn and Walter Skaggs?"

"Emily Conn was in the trailer with her parents. They were tied to the chairs at the dinner table and were all pretty beat up, but not a one of them would say what happened other than they'd hold themselves accountable to God."

"What about Dirty?"

"He wasn't there," Stewart said.

****

As he approached the Red Tin's open front door, Kevin realized it was not completely dark inside. He stepped through the threshold and stood before the candlelit dinner table. The soft, ruddy glow of the flickering flames striped Kate's naked body. She lay longways on the table with her arms outstretched, her hands hanging loosely off the sides. Tealight candles lined her body, a flickering cross with a shadow-laced woman strung upon it.

Kevin followed the outline to the head of the table. There sat JJ Conn with his elbows on the table, one on each side of Kate's head, his face hard, sanguinary, and his hands clasped together, fingers interlaced.

"Sit down, *Doctor* Ballard." His words sinuous and not far from a whisper.

Kevin stood there, a step inside the sill, with his mouth open and his eyes wide.

"Sit," JJ Conn repeated.

Kevin pulled out the chair at the foot of the table and sat. He looked across Kate's naked body to the head of the table and JJ Conn.

"Do you know why you find yourself here tonight, Doctor?" he asked, raising his eyebrows and tilting his head slightly.

Kevin couldn't find any words. His mouth felt full of a liquid sand.

JJ Conn nodded his head, and a guise of parental understanding covered his face.

"It's hard, I know. Repentance ain't something that comes easily." His head righted, the mask off.

"See, I was outside Chattanooga when I was a teenager, not much more than a boy really, traveling with Brother David Gilliam, formerly of West Virginia.

He's the one who taught me to read the leaves, see through the verses. See, a few weeks back, God showed me the path I was to take. I was to bring the Light. But I still *desired* to heal, you see. Desired.

"I felt so powerful when I put my hands on 'em and felt the Good Lord's power rush through my fingertips like lightning rods. I kept right on faith healing, despite the instruction of the work I was to do." His head jerked left to right in short, quick snaps. "That night, outside Chattanooga, I laid hands on a boy of twelve. He was a sufferer of seizures. Well, his eyes rolled back to the whites, and his teeth clamped down like a pond snapper and out flopped his tongue onto the sawdust. I couldn't feel a thing in my hands but that boy's jerking head. I let him go and knew the Lord was teaching me a lesson. See, I had mistaken His power as my own. I'd become drunk on it, and that boy lost his life to set me on my path, my current path, which led me directly to you.

"You know I've been waiting on you. She said she'd prefer the change to come on its own, your mother did. She had waited, too, you see."

Kevin was watching Kate's chest. He couldn't tell if it was rising and falling at first but, as his eyes adjusted, Kevin deciphered the undulation of her breath from the flickering light and the darting shadows.

She's alive, he thought.

"Always learning and never able to arrive at a knowledge of the truth," JJ Conn said.

Kevin looked up at the man.

"Ain't that the path you've chosen, *doctor*?"

"I don't know what you're talking about."

"Yes, you do. You've chosen to turn your back on

God and spit on the blood of Jesus Christ, who died for your sins. It's time to pay for your sins, doctor."

JJ Conn pushed himself to his feet, his chair toppling back and smacking the wooden floor. From behind Kate's head on the table, JJ Conn picked up a slender fishing fillet knife.

"Heaven is a far way away, and getting there, sometimes, comes at a price. There is always sacrifice. 'Go and cry out to the gods whom you have chosen; let them save you in the time of your distress,'" JJ Conn said, then slid the knife across Kate's bare throat.

Kevin lunged forward and tried to stop the flow of blood with his hands. Kate's eyes opened, wild in pain and confusion. They found Kevin's and held them briefly, then her struggling stopped and her eyes saw no more.

****

Kinders dug around in the glove box and found a cell phone charger. He hooked it to Ballard's phone, but it wouldn't come on until it had charged for a few moments. Kinders stood beside the open passenger door of the vehicle, which was still running, and looked from the phone to the Red Tin Cabin's open door.

The phone restarted and Kinders quickly called 911.

****

Stewart had pulled over to let Terry move to the front of the car.

Terry sat down and shut the door. Stewart moved the car forward, off the shoulder, and back onto the road.

The radio informed the men that JJ Conn had been reported at the Red Tin Cabin. A Jason Kinders had called and said one Kevin Ballard had went inside to confront JJ Conn.

"Turn the fucking car around," Terry said.

****

The lady on the phone told Kinders to stay where he was. She told him not to confront JJ Conn. She said help was on the way and to remain calm.

Ballard's scream tore from the Red Tin Cabin's open door and sent a torrent of icy needles down Kinders' spine. It was anguished and long and reverberated off the surrounding forest before fleeing across the valleys and escaping into the night.

Kinders tossed the phone onto the seat and ran toward the cabin. At the door, he slowed and tried the switch on the wall as he entered. The lights didn't come on, but he saw the table was littered with candles. Ballard stood over Katherine Johnson's naked body. Ballard yelled for Kinders to help him.

Kinders rushed to his side and saw the blood, black and glistening in the gloaming of the candle's feeble light. For a second, he thought she was just covered in shadows but just for a second. Then he saw.

Her throat was cut, and her blood covered the table and floor. Her eyes were open, but Kinders could see that she was gone.

Kinders wrapped his arms around Ballard and pulled him away from the table. Ballard fought against him, howling. The men slipped in the blood and fell to the floor. Kinders kept Ballard enfolded in his arms and scooted them away from the table and Katherine Johnson's body into a sitting position with his back against the wall. He held Ballard tightly and shushed him. Kinders told him that she was gone. Kinders told him that it was over, calm down, it was over.

Ballard ceased his struggle and succumbed to the tears.

****

They could see the lights flashing from the main road. Stewart slung the cruiser across the creek and up onto the ridge, where he had to immediately lock it up to avoid smashing into the back of an open ambulance, sending the paramedic leaning against it jumping off to the side. Another state car had pulled up behind Ballard's SUV. A sheriff's patrol car behind that, then the ambulance.

Stewart and Terry got out as Mullens came out the front door. He saw them approaching and stepped off the porch to meet them.

"Terry, you all right?" Mullens asked.

"Is he here? Was the Johnson girl with him?" Terry asked.

Mullens shook his head and said, "Conn was gone by the time I got here. He slit the girl's throat and cut out the backdoor."

"Jesus Christ," Terry said. "What about Ballard?"

"Dr. Ballard came in and confronted Conn. Said he cut her throat in front of him. There's a seven-inch fillet knife on the back porch, beside the hot tub."

Terry's head felt full of drowsy bees. He tried to shake them out, but that sent the world tilting.

"You all right, Terry?" Stewart asked.

"Yeah. I just need to sit down and rest a minute."

Terry let himself be led to the rocking chair on the porch. He sat with his eyes closed, his hands clasped around the chair's armrests. He took controlled, deep breaths and felt the dizzy spell leaving him.

Faintly, muffled by the walls and the noise of the first responders, Terry picked out the despairing sound of Kevin Ballard sobbing.

Chapter Thirteen

"No sign of him."
"Shit."
"Roadblocks?"
"Yep."
"Nothing."
"Nothing?"
"Nothing."
"Shit."
"We'll keep looking."
"Damn right, you will."

Shafts of illumination fought back the darkness around the Red Tin. The sound of men breathing heavily and cursing among the snapping of twigs and the crunching of bootheels. The crackle and hiss of handheld radios and the distant cries of coyotes. The echo of a dog's whine, then its bark.

****

The light, crisp, white, and blinding, made Terry's stomach upset. A wave of nausea and dizziness enveloped him, sweat prickling his forehead, neck, and arms.

"You've got quite a concussion," the doctor said.

There was a click and the light vanished, leaving a blinding ghost of itself that traced its way across Terry's vision.

"I'd say you're going to miss, at least, a week of

work, Detective," the doctor said. "I'll know more once we do the scan."

"Shit."

"No, shit. You've got a serious knock there. You're going to need to take it easy and allow yourself some time to heal."

"Can't," Terry said, sliding down off the paper-covered examination table. "No rest for the wicked and all that."

As Terry retrieved his jacket from the coatrack, he saw the doctor, shaking his head and making notes.

"It would be best if you didn't share any of this with my supervisor," Terry said. "Doctor/patient confidentiality and all."

The doctor sighed and made some feeble arguments about a physician's duty to the public and those serving it, but Terry knew he'd keep his mouth shut.

****

Stewart was talking to a nurse in the waiting room.

"How's the noggin?" he asked.

"Fine," Terry said. "Let's get back at it."

As the door opened into the darkened parking lot, Terry had to slow his gait and strain his eyes to see only one set of Stewart's shined boots striding in front of him.

****

They set up roadblocks and formed armed search parties. Dozens of men and women with guns, flashlights, and stern faces. They combed the area around the Red Tin Cabin again and again, but JJ Conn was nowhere to be found. Someone said the Boogie Man had slipped back under the bed. They plastered the bastard's face across the news outlets. APBs were issued. The FBI was consulted. All the steps of protocol and procedure were carried out, but the man was a ghost.

"He'll turn up," Polk said. "Somebody'll rat on him."

Terry nodded his head, once, and regretted it. The office swam and smeared, and for a horrified instance, Terry was sure he was going to vomit in his sergeant's office. The feeling passed, and Terry did his best to keep his face stony and unreadable.

"You ok, Terry?" Polk asked.

It was weird hearing the man ask the question.

Terry forced a wan smile.

"Nothing a good cup of black coffee won't fix," he said.

****

"Want to head back up Black Creek?" Stewart asked.

"Doubt he'll be up that way for a while."

"Well."

Terry tapped his hand on his thigh, a tool of distraction for the pinpricks of pain erupting in his temples. The headache swelled, then receded every thirty minutes or so.

"What do you want to do?" Stewart asked.

"Give me a goddamn minute, will you?" Terry said through clenched teeth.

He could see his pulse in the peripheries of his sight. Twin sets of pounding that shimmered and shook. He closed his eyes and focused on his breathing.

Slow. In. Out. In. Out.

Terry heard the office door open and close. He

cautiously allowed his eyes to open, the harsh florescent lights glaring and painful. Stewart had gone.

In. Out.

Where's the bastard gone? Where's he going?

Terry thought as he sat back in the chair.

****

The buzzing of his cellphone in his pocket woke him. Terry jerked up and, instantly, felt sick. His head pounded; he was covered in a cold, oily sweat.

Shit, he thought. *I was asleep.*

Terry tried to read the phone's screen, but his eyes refused to focus. The colors of the screen vibrated, drifted into each other until it was a crayon impressionistic piece, some ten-year-old Monet's attempt at an office. The phone buzzed again in his hand, and the sound seemed abnormally loud. An angry hornets' nest buzzing.

Terry slid his finger across the screen, an action he'd taken a hundred times, to accept the call. He closed his eyes at the brightness of the room and pressed the speaker to his ear.

"Hello?"

"Trooper Terry."

The voice was slow, sure, and methodic. Terry could hear the curling of the lips into a smile as it spoke, a sound both obscene and frightening.

"How's the head?" JJ Conn asked.

Terry, against all the strength and resolve he could muster, leaned over and vomited into the trashcan beside his desk.

****

Kevin Ballard did not bow his head when the preacher instructed the funeral crowd to do so. He stood there under the bright blue sky and hot sun and watched the breeze ruffle the leaflets of a lavender rose in the casket spray on Kate's coffin. A short time later, a consort of subdued *amens* exhaled into the afternoon air. He hadn't heard a single word of it.

Kate's mother and father, whom he'd dined with on a handful of occasions in Lexington, held each other close and wept openly. Kevin couldn't look at them.

The preacher opened his small Bible and read, "Peace I leave with you; my peace I give you. I do not give to you as the world gives. Do not let your hearts be troubled and do not be afraid."

The preacher closed the Bible and thanked those in attendance for paying their respects to Katherine and her family.

Peace? What peace have you left for me? Kevin wondered. *How can my heart not be troubled? How the hell can I be nothing but afraid? Anything but at peace? A psychopath murdered my mother and my girlfriend, an old man who told us about some asinine hoodoo, and probably a girl working at a gas station for the hell of it, too. Who knows how many others there are. You do not give to me as the world gives? If you exist, created everything, then why...*

He was brought from his thoughts by the shuffling of starched clothes and shoes crushing manicured lawn. The funeral party was dissipating, heading back to their homes or jobs, life as normal sans one graduate college girl.

Kevin walked over to Mr. and Mrs. Johnson and woodenly offered his condolences for the umpteenth time. The words were useless, meaningless, a drop from a bucket in the ocean of grief, jet black loss. But it was all he had to offer. He shook Mr. Johnson's hand and kissed Mrs. Johnson's tear-soaked cheek, then walked back to his vehicle and sat behind the wheel.

He didn't start it right away. He sat there and did his best to control his tears.

When it had passed, Kevin turned the key in the ignition and left.

****

Emmanuel Stephens's office was in Elizabethtown, some twenty miles from Kevin's parents' house, his house. Kevin drove down yesterday after Kate's funeral and spent most of the night on the deck overlooking the Nolin River. He sat up long after the sun went down and watched the stars cross the clear sky. That night, he dreamt of Kate's smiling face and the music of her laughter.

Kevin pulled into the office building fifteen minutes early and consulted the directory; the building housed a dentist, an insurance company call center, and several other lawyers aside from the Hon. E. Stephens. Kevin walked into Mr. Stephens's small office on the second floor and found that Mr. Stephens didn't have a secretary. There was an uncomfortable-looking couch, a small table with a coffee pot, spoon, and sugar, then a door leading to another room. Kevin crossed to the other room, knocked on the doorsill, and entered.

Mr. Stephens sat behind the desk, scrupulously working on what appeared to be a handwritten letter. He didn't look up from the letter.

"Come in, Dr. Ballard. Come in."

There was a leather armchair in front of the desk. Kevin sat in it and looked around the office. There were several high bookcases overflowing with books, mostly on law, but Kevin saw a few legal thrillers in the mix. Kevin saw two framed Audubon prints, one on each side of the room. On the left wall was the Great Cinereous Owl: a regal, tenured professor about to impart a nugget of wisdom from his wealth of erudition. On the right, the Great Horned Owl: the weary, cross-eyed woodsmen approached by the crafty outsider.

The window behind Mr. Stephens looked out onto the parking lot and the loading dock of the *News-Enterprise* just beyond. Kevin watched two workers on their smoke break while Mr. Stephens wrote. They leaned against the building and laughed, the blue smoke tendrils lazily drifting upward and dissipating.

Kevin didn't feel a bit annoyed at having to wait. Kevin filled his head with welcome nothing for the first time in what seemed like years and sat there in it for the few moments before Mr. Stephens spoke.

"I appreciate you coming in today, Dr. Ballard," Mr. Stephens said, carefully folding the paper into thirds.

"I'm sorry I missed our previous appointment."

"Your mother left you the house and the land and some stocks and money, of course, but there was one item that she said had to be hand delivered to you by me. I hadn't even had time to properly file it," he said.

Mr. Stephens stuffed the folded page into an envelope and dropped it onto his desk. He then pulled out a drawer and shuffled its contents about. He brought out a small silver key. Mr. Stephens held the key between his thumb, fore, and middle fingers.

"Here it is."

He reached across the desk and handed it to Kevin, who turned it over in his palm. It looked unassuming, a normal little lock key.

"What's it for?"

"She said it goes to a safe she has in the house, but she didn't specify exactly where in the house it was. I assume she thought she would have more time to plan these things. She'd come in only a few weeks before, well, you know what, to draft the will. Anyway, I don't think she would've hidden it," Mr. Stephens said.

Kevin couldn't see his mother sneaking about the house with a cashbox, pulling open hidden compartments behind pictures.

"I don't either," Kevin said. "Did she tell you what's in the safe? This all sounds too secretive for my mother."

"No." Mr. Stephens opened another drawer of his desk and pulled out a thick manila folder. "Let's get on to the paperwork, shall we?"

Kevin took the Western Kentucky Parkway back home. The sun burned orange in the purpling sky, and he drove the twenty minutes in silence. He tried to hold on to the nothingness while it still sat in his head. He didn't want to think about Kate. His mother. JJ Conn. The old man at the Store. The girl at the gas station. The research left undone. The Biology Department.

He set the cruise control just under eighty and chased the sun toward the horizon and his parents' empty house.

****

Kevin didn't look for the safe that night. He turned the television on to some science-fiction movie and opened all the windows on the first floor. He slid open the deck doors and sat in one of the cushioned chairs. The moon had begun its slow slide across the night sky.

It reflected off the slow-moving Nolin, just down the hill.

Kevin woke the next morning to the sound of his cell phone ringer. He reached toward the nightstand for the phone but knocked it off. It fell to the floor and rang from somewhere under the bed.

"Jesus," Kevin said, stretching in the bed.

He closed his eyes and was just drifting back off to sleep when the voice mail notification dinged.

Kevin opened his eyes and slid out of the covers. He stood and stretched, then fell to his knees at the bedside. He reached under the bed, and his hand brushed cold steel, sending goosebumps rippling across his body. He craned his head down and saw the phone sitting next to a small metal box. He pulled both items from underneath the bed.

The phone call was from an unknown number. Kevin tossed the phone onto the covers and sat on the edge of the bed with the box. He turned it over and slid his fingers across the keyhole. He set the box on the bed and walked down the hall into the kitchen and retrieved the key from the manila folder on the counter. He walked back to the bedroom and got back into bed. He sat, leaned against the headboard with the cold metal box on his bare stomach. He fitted the key into the keyhole and opened it.

The box contained a brown, leather-bound diary and an old photograph of his mother and father holding Kevin, then a naked, wet baby, dripping from his baptism seconds before. His mother and father looked smilingly into the camera lens. Baby Kevin was in mid-wail, obviously not happy about being plunged into the cold, unfamiliar water.

Kevin set the empty box and the photo aside. He brought the leather diary before him and undid the straps. Kevin hadn't known his mother to keep a diary, much less one in a lock box under her bed. He pinched the bulk of pages at the corner and flipped through them like an animated flip book from his childhood. Page after page of handwritten black ink whirred by. Kevin opened the diary to the first page and read.

The first entry didn't have a date. In it his mother wrote about how excited she and Jim were to have baby Kevin baptized the following day at Grandma Margot's Nazarene church in rural Grayson County. She wrote that, though Jim and herself had believers' baptisms, they feared something could happen to their baby before he was old enough to speak the words for himself. She said she let Grandma Margot arrange for the baptism, but she fully expected Kevin to say "I believe" when he reached adulthood.

His mother thanked God for her baby boy as if the diary were not a diary but a direct letter to God. The style switched back and forth from diary to letter. Kevin's mother described the joy of holding her baby boy for the first time, the look of loving adoration on Jim's face when he held Kevin.

Kevin couldn't help but feel surprised by the religiosity of the diary. He'd always known of his parents' devoted beliefs, but he hadn't really taken it seriously until reading the diary. He'd had discussions with his parents, at their insistence, but he found that he had put up some blinders to his parents' religiousness because it hurt to think about their dated dependence on a spirit world.

They'd sat him down several times, very much like

an intervention, and told him that they were scared for his soul. They told him that they knew he was a good person, but being a good person wasn't always enough. He needed to accept Jesus Christ as his personal Lord and Savior. His parents told him it was nice that he had such a fascinating career in science and that he valued education and learning, but he needed to reevaluate what he held in the highest esteem. He needed Jesus.

Kevin had never come to fully understand either of his parents' beliefs. He knew them to be very intelligent people, so he couldn't understand why they'd thrown in the towel and committed what he came to believe was intellectual suicide. It was easier to try and avoid the subject and not think about it.

Holding the leather-bound diary, Kevin found he could no longer ignore it.

****

Kevin put a shirt on and took the diary into the kitchen with him. He made a pot of coffee and sat down at the table to read. A quick skim of the thing showed that his mother didn't add to the diary every day; entries were not about the mundane things of her daily routine.

He left the diary open on the table and set about opening all the windows on the first floor. The cool morning air filled the house, and through the windows, the sunshine poured in.

Kevin sat back down at the table with the diary and his coffee in hand.

Monday, Sept. 17, 1990: Today Kevin's teacher called. Mrs. Thomas said Kevin was cussing another student during an altercation stemming from an eraser. She said the other child had started the incident and was being punished for his role, but Kevin was going to be put in in-school detention for his language and handling of the thing. We scheduled a parent-teacher conference for Wednesday.

When Kevin got off the bus, I was waiting for him on the couch. He opened the door, and his face was sullen. I sat him down beside me and asked him if there was something he wanted to tell me. He just sat there for a moment; then, all at once, he said he had gotten in trouble at school for saying words he wasn't supposed to say because Timothy took his eraser and said he wasn't giving it back. I let Kevin tell all he was going to tell.

When he was done, I asked him if he'd handled the situation the way Jesus would have handled it. He sat there and shook his head, looking at his feet. I asked him how he thought he could have handled the situation in a more Christian way. Kevin said he could have handled the situation better by not getting angry, yelling, and cussing. Kevin said he should have raised his hand and had Mrs. Thomas assist him in getting his eraser back.

He didn't say it would have been a more Christian way to handle it; he said "better." I thought about addressing that with him then but decided that that might be a little too much on his plate for one day. Besides, he expressed regret for having said the things he had said, as well as for the anger he expressed.

In the margin of this entry, in handwriting that did not resemble his mother's or his father's, written in red ink was *Proverbs 22:6*.

Kevin got up from the table and walked back to the bedroom and returned to the kitchen with his cell phone. He sat back down at the table and looked up

Proverbs 22:6.

"Train a child in the way he should go, and when he is old, he will not turn from it," Kevin read.

Kevin vaguely recalled that fifth-grade incident. The kid had taken the eraser from his desk quickly and made faces at him, telling him he wasn't getting it back. He'd taunted, "Dumbass. Dumbass," until Kevin had had it. He jumped up from his desk and started grappling with the kid for the eraser. The teacher quickly separated them, and Kevin had felt like he was filled to bursting with rage. He screamed at the kid while the teacher held him back, calling him "a shit" over and over again.

Kevin smiled at the image of himself so young and so angry, screaming "shit" in elementary school. He hadn't thought about that in years. Then Kevin remembered feeling so ashamed of himself for losing control. He had to listen to the teacher, the principal, his mother, and his father lecture him about the same incident.

Kevin scanned the entry, then its marginalia again, looking for any clues as to its author. He didn't find anything except the red *Proverbs 22:6.*

Kevin read on.

****

Kevin read several more entries, none of which had any red ink in the margins. The entries seemed so trivial to Kevin—Kevin stubs his toe and says "Goddamit" and his mother hears. She tells Kevin not to take the Lord's name in vain and Kevin apologizes. His mother sees Kevin looking off into the distance while the rest of the baseball team's heads are bowed, their lips reciting the Lord's Prayer.

With each entry, Kevin could see the pattern more clearly. The brown, leather-bound diary was a list of his sins, his fleeting faith, that his mother felt responsible for his lack of. His sins. Her failures. Inescapable sadness swooned inside him.

Did his mother die believing she was a failed parent? That she failed her God?

****

"Francine and little Abigail send their regards, Trooper Terry."

Terry couldn't breathe. He wiped the phlegmy vomit from his lips and chin, sweat streaking down his forehead and stinging down into his eyes.

"What have you done?" Terry whispered.

It was all he could manage. He tried to open his eyes and stand, but the room swam, and Terry sank back into the chair behind his desk.

"The Lord's work," JJ Conn said.

His voice was gentle, almost musical.

"I'll kill you," Terry whispered, "if you've touched so much as a hair on either of their heads. Kill you."

JJ Conn's laugh was the rustling of briars in the night, the fox slipping between the low-lying trees, hen in mouth.

"It looks like Francine fared better than you did in the divorce," Conn said. "Come alone."

The line went dead.

****

The diary became increasingly more difficult to read. This did not have anything to do with the handwriting or the syntax of the thing; it was his mother's guilty conscience. With each entry, it bled onto the page, and she saw every missed opportunity to save Kevin's soul as another failure heaped up in her opprobrious pile.

Kevin felt he had led a good life. He contributed to society, the ever-expanding confines of the human understanding of the environment. He did no wrong that he could see, yet his life had brought his mother such a tremendous amount of ignominy. Kevin had never felt embarrassment for his existence and couldn't see any reason why he should.

The diary made him sick to his stomach. He wished his mother were sitting before him, so he could tell her that it was all bullshit. There was no shining gate waiting for anyone when they died. You lived and then you died. That was it. So why waste your time and energy on regret?

Kevin's anger receded, and he felt tired, so tired.

****

Kevin made another pot of coffee and sat out on the deck in the sunshine while it brewed. He left the diary on the dinner table. He closed his eyes and tilted his face toward the sun. He slowed his breathing and reclined back into the chair.

Proverbs 22:6.

Repent, Sinner.

Kevin opened his eyes and sat up in the chair, his jaw clenched, teeth ground. He rubbed his eyes and went back into the kitchen and made himself another cup of coffee. He sat back down at the table and continued reading his mother's diary.

****

Kevin worked his way up into his mid-twenties. His mother fretted about his growing love of and studying of science, especially evolution. The word was dug into the paper, for the length of the word, like the pen's weight suddenly tripled.

He'd stopped his church attendance as soon as he moved away from home. Kevin didn't see the point in keeping up appearances when he didn't even reside in the same house as his parents. For the first couple of semesters, he'd lied to his mother and father when they called or visited and told them he went to the on-campus Baptist ministries at Western Kentucky University.

Kevin figured they'd known that he'd stopped going to church but felt obligated to ask anyway, their Christian duty. One fall weekend, they came down to Bowling Green to visit, and they'd picked him up from his dorm. They were driving to Theresa's for lunch, Kevin toying with his phone in the backseat, and his mother said the place looked nice. Kevin looked up and asked what she was talking about. Kevin saw they were passing the church he was supposedly attending. He was too quick in correcting himself, saying that, yes, it was a nice place and he enjoyed it greatly.

They'd stopped asking him after that trip.

The entries confirmed his suspicions. He read about how his mother felt Kevin was keeping something from her, and she thought he was lying about attending service. She wrote about how her baby was no longer a child, and she hoped she had instilled enough goodness in him to last him the rest of his life, as if there was a line somewhere inside of him, as if all she had to do was put just enough of this "goodness" to surpass that line, then he'd be okay and have enough in him to coast to the finish line.

The entries were progressively lamenting. His

mother reflected on past chances to "save Kevin's soul." She wished she had been more forceful. Maybe Kevin would have had Faith—she capitalized the "F" every time she wrote the word—if she'd been more cogent. Kevin sped through the entries with more cursoriness. His mother began talking to Pastor Cessaurs about her concerns. Pastor C, as he was referred to in his mother's shorthand, told her to pray without ceasing and to focus on the good she had instilled in Kevin. Some enter the flock later in life than others, he'd said.

Kevin turned the page and came upon a folded sheet of Xeroxed paper. He unfolded it and found that it was a flyer with tear-off tabs. The header, in emboldened capital letters, read: THERE IS A LIGHT IN THE DARK! Next was a quote from Corinthians, chapter six, verse fourteen: "Do not be unequally yoked with unbelievers. For what partnership has righteousness with lawlessness? Or what fellowship has light with darkness?" The flyer asked the reader if someone they loved rejected Christ. The flyer asked, What would the reader do to help their loved one find the light in the dark?

The flyer said you could only do so much before you turned to "the Anointed" for assistance. The flyer said the Anointed could help all those that the Good Lord had deemed worthy turn their faces to the light and open their closed eyes. The flyer quoted Proverbs, chapter twenty-four, verse twenty: "For the evil man has no future; the lamp of the wicked will be put out."

The flyer said the Anointed had years of experience assisting the family and friends of unbelievers open their eyes to the Truth. The flyer closed with a quote from Timothy, chapter five, verse eight: "But if anyone does not provide for his relatives, and especially members of his household, he has denied the faith and is worse than an unbeliever." Four of the nine tabs on the flyer had been removed. The tabs read "The Anointed" and had a telephone number with a 606 area code, eastern Kentucky. Nowhere on the flyer was there the name or names of "the Anointed."

Kevin turned back to the diary and read.

Sunday, October 26, 2014: Pastor C came up to me today after the service. He took me back into his office and closed the door. He took a flyer off his desk and handed it to me. He told me someone had brought several of these flyers to the church and, as soon as he saw what they were about, he had thought of me. I read the flyer and couldn't help but cry. Pastor C, he told me not to cry and that if there were people doing what the flyer proclaimed that meant I wasn't the only one in my position. Pastor C told me to think and pray on it for a few days. I left his office feeling hopeful.

Kevin shook his head, feeling sick to his stomach. He read the next entry.

Wednesday, October 29, 2014: I called the number on the flyer today. No one answered, but I left a voice mail message. I put the phone down, feeling silly, and it rang back almost immediately. A soft-spoken man named Jeremiah Jeffrey apologized for missing my call and asked if he could help me. I told him that I hoped so and said it was about my son, Kevin.

I told him about it. He was quiet, but I could tell he was listening. I could feel it somehow. I was blubbering like a baby by the time I finished.

Jeremiah Jeffrey asked me if I was willing to do

whatever it took to get Kevin right with God. I told him I was, of course, I was. He asked for my address and for Kevin's phone number and home address. I felt my stomach knot up at Kevin getting a call from a strange man his mother sicced on him, but Jeremiah Jeffrey said for me not to worry. He wouldn't contact Kevin until he learned more about us and then only after I was sure I wanted his assistance.

Kevin pushed up from the table, sending the chair crashing back onto the hardwood floor with a smack. Jeremiah Jeffrey.

Conn.

God.

Chapter Fourteen

Everything was reeling, spinning. Kevin sat down on the floor. He pulled his legs in, Indian-style, and held his head with his hands.

Repent, Sinner.

Kevin looked up at the table and saw his mother's lifeless body, the blood, and the candles. Light and dark, life and death. All the carnage stemmed from his mother's insecurity about her parenting and something illusory and most likely fabricated, his soul and its eternal destination.

Willing to do whatever it took to get Kevin right with God.

"Jesus Christ," Kevin whispered.

****

Kevin pulled himself to his feet and dug his cell phone out of his pocket. He unlocked the screen, opened up his contact list, and found Detective David Terry, but he didn't place the call. His thumb hovered over the call button for a moment. Then he locked the screen and slid the phone back into his pocket.

Kevin stood with both hands on the table and looked down at his mother's diary and the unfolded flyer. He made up his mind. He was going to read the diary in its entirety before calling Det. Terry and giving it over to them as evidence, the only lead that hadn't grown cold.

Kevin righted the chair and sat down in it. He scooted himself up to the table, then carefully folded the flyer back and tucked it into the fold of the diary. He turned the page and read.

****

Their first meeting was that Friday, October 31st, Halloween.

How fitting, Kevin thought. *This is madness.*

He shook his head and shuttered. Kevin couldn't help feeling like an agent from the Better Business Bureau sent out to investigate a vulture preying on the elderly; except, instead of pension checks and social security, this vulture took lives and dignity.

They met at the Captain D's on Dixie Highway in Elizabethtown.

His mother wrote:

Jeremiah Jeffrey is a very large man. He is tall as a tree and looks as sturdy. He wore very plain clothes, a loose-fitting T-shirt and a very worn pair of blue jeans. His head was shaved bald, and his skin was very pale. He was sitting at a booth on the far side of the restaurant that faced the door. He saw me come in and I saw him looking. I walked right over to him and sat down.

His voice was just like it sounded on the phone, soft and calm. Jeremiah Jeffrey said that he had consulted with God, and it had been decided that he would take my case. It was weird to hear it like that, but he asked me a lot of questions about Kevin and how I'd raised him, how I'd disciplined him, which church had I taken him to, had I always taken him to that church, had Kevin ever said anything about church or religion in a negative manner. I answered all those questions and then some. I can't even recall half of everything he asked me. Jeremiah Jeffrey spoke with a long drawl, but it seemed like those questions were fired one after the other. He said he would do some looking into Kevin but would not disturb him or alert him as to his work. He said he'd call, and we'd have another meeting in about a week's time.

Kevin's chest felt tight. He put his hands on his head to open his lungs and did his best to breathe deeply, but it came in and out, shaky and shallow. He'd never been able to fully articulate his feelings, and the mixture that hit him then was staggering in its complication. He was angry, scared, sad, appalled, and tired, so tired.

It was strange that he had this diary in his hands that held so many pieces to the puzzle, but it was nearly impossible to force himself to read another line. Kevin wanted to curl up and sleep for the next thirty years. Maybe not even wake up then, just keep right on sleeping until he fell into the Big Sleep.

Kevin stood up and made another pot of coffee. He took each of the actions involved slowly, deliberately. He emptied the carafe, placed a new filter with fresh grounds into the maker, then poured in the water. A half moment later, Kevin smelled the coffee brewing and found a line back to the resolve he'd had earlier. He was going to get through that goddamn diary. He was going to understand why the pieces of the puzzle were warped and not fitting quite right. He owed it to Kate. He owed it to himself, too.

****

"Terry. Terry," Stewart shouted. "Where are you going?"

Terry did his best impression of a straight-line march across the room, toward the hall. He felt straight-armed drunk, walking rigid and unsure, like some reanimated mummy. Terry weaved, the lights and faces and desks and chairs blurring together, then reeling off in different directions, and caught his foot on a chair. He tripped and knew he was going to fall.

Stewart caught him by the arm, just as Terry was going down.

"Easy, man," Stewart said. "Jesus. You don't look good."

Terry closed his eyes and swallowed back acid. He was covered in sweat, his clothes clinging to him, cold and soaked. "He called me."

"Who?" Stewart answered his own question. "JJ Conn. Jesus. When?"

"Just now."

"What'd he say?"

"He's got Abi and Francine. At Francine's place."

"Shit," Stewart said, releasing Terry's arm. "I'll tell—"

"No." Terry jerked his eyes open. "Not Polk, not anybody. He's got my little girl."

Stewart's eyes were wide and conflicted, but he eventually nodded.

****

Tuesday, November 18, 2014: Jeremiah Jeffrey called this afternoon. He said he needed to meet with me and discuss the plan for Kevin's Salvation. We set it up so that he'll meet me at the church about an hour after the service tomorrow night. We'd use one of the rec rooms. It'd save him driving all the way to the house, and it was closer to the highway.

Wednesday, November 19, 2014: I was waiting in the hall when Jeremiah Jeffrey came through the doors. Everybody had been cleared out for quite a while. I led him to the room, and we both sat down at the table. He was different. He looked at me with this smile, a smirk almost. He didn't say anything out and out mean or nasty or anything like that, but it was like he held me in some sort of contempt.

He said he'd looked more thoroughly into Doctor Kevin Ballard. He said the word "doctor" like it was poisonous. He said he'd never had a case such as this. Jeremiah Jeffrey said it would require a lot of doing. He smiled a little wider when he said that last part. He said he enjoyed a challenge and that all things are possible through God. He said he had some more work to do and that he would contact me again for another meeting. I started to ask him about payment, which we had yet to discuss, but he was already up on his feet and out the door.

The more Kevin read, the more he felt like Alice falling down the rabbit hole. His mother's entries became more and more self-critical. She mentioned several more phone calls with JJ Conn over the next few months.

She also wrote about a phone call she and Kevin had in which she told him that she wished he would come visit some weekend and that maybe they could go to church together one Sunday, like they used to. She wrote about the silence and the static on the other side of the line that was eventually filled with a "sure, Mom." Kevin's mother wrote that she had failed, missed her opportunity some years ago, and that it was out of her control now. She felt that Jeremiah Jeffrey was her only hope of saving Kevin's soul.

There wasn't even a mention of Kevin finding Jesus on his own. Kevin was embarrassed at the stab of resentment he felt about that, like he was lacking some ability to behold some great truth in the grand scheme of things, a boy of six not understanding calculus.

****

Thursday, January 1, 2015: I met with Jeremiah Jeffrey at the Captain D's this afternoon. He told me that things were about to start proceeding with more motion. He asked me if I was prepared to do whatever it takes to get Kevin right with God. I told him that I was, that I had already told him that I was, and that I was upset about him asking me that every time we spoke. Jeremiah Jeffrey stopped me by raising his big hand and cocking his head to the side, like a dog trying to understand what you're telling it. He said there would be some hard truths in this process and that I had the lion's share of the guilt involved. He didn't say it with malice. He just said it and it was enough.

Jeremiah Jeffrey let me cry there until I was about all cried out. People looked over at us there in the booth and then went back to their food. I dried my eyes and said I had to take what responsibility was mine. He nodded his head real slow and leaned down across the table, and I looked up. He's a very large man, and he asked me if I was familiar with the Book of Deuteronomy. I nodded my head, and he asked if I could recall chapter twenty-four, verse sixteen. I shook my head. I couldn't recall that particular chapter and verse off the top of my head.

Jeremiah Jeffrey said it right there in the booth without any hesitation; he just spit out the words. I looked it up on my phone as soon as I got back in my car, and he didn't miss a word of it: "Fathers shall not be put to death because of their children, nor shall children be put to death because of their fathers. Each one shall be put to death for his own sin."

Jeremiah Jeffrey said it, word for word, then sat back against the booth with a deliberate smile that about broke my heart for what it knew.

****

Kevin realized he was grinding his teeth. His fists were compact balls of white knuckles sitting on both sides of the diary. He looked up at the clock and saw it was late. His mind absently said he should go to bed, but he knew he wouldn't be able to sleep until he'd finished with the diary. Kevin saw his mother's face wet with tears and wished that Jeremiah Jeffrey Conn would knock on his front door.

****

Kevin felt his phone vibrating in his pocket, but he ignored it. He kept reading.

Tuesday, January 6, 2015: Jeremiah Jeffrey called this morning. He said the more inquiry he put into Kevin, the more he sees his Salvation as an uphill battle that is going to require a great deal of sacrifice to achieve, if not the direct interference of the Lord Almighty. He said Kevin had published many papers and articles in science journals regarding the Great Lie, evolution.

Jeremiah Jeffrey asked me if Kevin was familiar with the Book of Genesis, like I'd never read the Bible to him. When I said that he was, that I'd read a great portion of the Good Book to Kevin during his childhood, Jeremiah Jeffrey snorted. I heard it clear as

A.S. Coomer

day over the line. He told me to look up Proverbs, chapter twenty-nine, verse fifteen and hung up. I got out my Bible and it read, "The rod and reproof give wisdom, but a child left to himself brings shame to his mother." *I felt so guilty that I couldn't bring myself to tell Jeremiah Jeffrey about* Nolin & the Hellbenders.

The red ink marginalia read: *Luke 8:17.*

Kevin got up from the table and walked over to the bookshelf in the living room. He squatted down and found his mother's Bible on the end, the easiest book to retrieve from the shelf. He took it over to the table and sat back down. He flipped to the table of contents, found the Book of Luke, and turned to chapter eight and verse seventeen.

Kevin read, "For nothing is hidden that will not be made manifest, nor is anything secret that will not be known and come to light."

Jeremiah Jeffrey Conn had written in his mother's diary. He was the red ink. Kevin felt sure after reading Luke 8:17 in his mother's Bible.

How did he get ahold of the diary? How did he know she kept one?

****

Terry gave Stewart directions to the house. They drove several miles in a charged silence before Stewart pulled the car to a stop a half-mile away.

"What're you doing?" Terry asked.

"Are you sure you're ok?" Stewart asked. "You don't look so good. Maybe we should call this in. Bring in Polk. Get SWAT from Pikeville or something."

"He's got my little girl, goddamn it."

"I know he said he does," Stewart said, "but what if he's lying? What if he doesn't and this is all just a trap or worse?"

"He doesn't lie," Terry said, shaking his head.

The nausea was slackening a bit. Terry guessed it was the adrenaline. He drew his firearm and flicked the safety off. "You either put this fucking car back in drive or I'm walking."

"Jesus."

Stewart killed the lights, then got the car back in motion.

****

Saturday, January 10, 2015: Jeremiah Jeffrey showed up at the house today. We hadn't planned a meeting, and he hadn't called beforehand. I was doing dishes and felt odd, and when I looked up, he was standing there, looking in the window at me. I jumped and spilled dishwater on the floor. I let him in and we sat down on the couch. He stared at me and I felt uncomfortable.

I asked him what brought him out to the house, and he asked if he could see my diary. I hadn't told him I kept one. I asked him how he knew about my diary, and he just asked me to give it to him.

I walked back to the bedroom and got it out of the lockbox and brought it back to the living room. I didn't sit back down on the couch. I stood there in front of the couch and held the diary out to him. He didn't take it right off but looked at me and said that he didn't think it was right.

I asked him what wasn't right, and he said that I was keeping things from him when he was trying to help Kevin and myself. I walked back into the kitchen and dried up the dishwater on the floor, then finished the dishes. Jeremiah Jeffrey sat there on the couch and read my diary.

When he had finished, he stood up and dropped the diary onto the coffee table. He said he had to "consult the leaves" about how he was going to proceed. He walked out the front door, and I saw his white truck go by in the window.

****

Tuesday, January 20, 2015: He was at the house when I pulled in from work, his white truck sitting there in the driveway. I walked over and looked to see if he was waiting in it, but he wasn't. I walked on down the path and went to put my key in the front door but decided to try it first, and it was unlocked. I opened it and called in.

No one answered, but when I stepped inside, I saw him sitting on the couch with his leg crossed at the ankle, reading my diary. He didn't look up or acknowledge me when I entered. I put my keys on the hook and my purse on the counter. I didn't know what to say. I stood there looking at him, but he just kept on reading. I turned a chair from the table and sat in it, facing him. We sat there in silence for a while; he kept reading and I watched him.

I noticed that he'd worn the same clothes he'd worn on our other meetings, the baggy T-shirt and worn blue jeans. He left my diary open on his lap and looked over at me. He shook his head, and there was no trace of a smile or kindness. He looked disappointed, like when you did something that embarrassed your mother in public.

Jeremiah Jeffrey stood up and said he understood why Kevin was the way he was. He said that enlisting his services was the most I'd ever done for Kevin. I felt that I should've gotten angry and cussed and thrown him out of the house but the fact that my first feeling was shame kept me from it.

I sat there in the chair, tears a-flowing and couldn't keep eye contact with him. He closed the diary and put it on the couch beside him. He stood up and said he had a lot of work to do yet and left. I sat there for half an hour in that chair at the dinner table and cried. I prayed to God to forgive me for being the fickle, weak mother that I am and to allow Kevin into Heaven. I promised God that I would take Kevin's place in Hell if God could just let my boy in.

After I composed myself, I picked up the diary and walked back to the bedroom. The lockbox was sitting on my bed with the lid open. The picture of Kevin's baptism was still in there, and I put the diary back in and closed it, then slid it back under the bed. I opened my jewelry box and found that my spare diary key was no longer in the pull-out drawer of earrings. I closed all the curtains but still couldn't shake the feeling that he was watching me.

****

The house was dark, not a single light shone. Even the floodlight attached to the garage was out.

"You take the front," Terry said, the interior layout of the house running through his mind. "I'll take the back, where the dining room is. I'll bet that's where they're at."

"Are you sure you're up for this, Terry?"

It was difficult, but Terry tore his eyes from his ex-wife's house and let them hold Stewart's. The other detective's eyes doubled, then slowly drifted back into a single set.

"Yes," Terry said. "I am. Are you?"

Stewart killed the engine.

"Let's go."

****

The night swam around him in dark currents. Terry stepped out onto the driveway, crouched, both hands on the gun. The air was cooler, a faint breeze bringing up goosebumps across his sweat-soaked body.

Please be ok. Abigail's sweet smiling face flickering in Terry's head like a television losing reception. *Please be ok. I'll kill him. Please be ok.*

Terry stepped up onto the back porch, leaned against the cold brick, and listened. His breathing came in ragged rasps, and he felt a shakiness, foreign and troubling, in every atom of his being. He heard nothing, save the lone warble from a nightjar somewhere nearby.

Terry took a deep breath, then swung his right foot with everything he had into the backdoor. It splintered the frame and shot inward, imbedding the doorknob into the wall.

"Abigail," Terry shouted into the darkness.

He flipped the light switch, but nothing happened.

"Abigail, where are you?"

He heard a muted crash, then Stewart's shouting from the front of the house.

"Police. Police."

Terry flicked his flashlight on. He trained the light on the kitchen table. There they were.

Oh, God.

****

Kevin turned the page and realized that he had about finished the thing. A thin sliver of pages remained. He looked up from the diary to the window.

He saw his reflection in the lamplight. Darkness covered everything outside, and Kevin could just barely make out the moon behind the dagger-like branches of the dogwood tree his mother had planted when he was twelve.

It was nearly three-thirty in the morning. Kevin hadn't eaten anything in hours; his stomach churned on cue. He got up and made himself toast and yet another pot of coffee. He sat back down at the table with his breakfast and continued reading.

Kevin's mother wrote that she should have listened to Jim, who she missed dearly, when he advised that they be more firm with Kevin, regarding his biblical learning. Jim wanted to enroll Kevin at St. Joseph's, instead of public school, even though they weren't Catholic. Jim said it would be good for Kevin to get a heavy dose of Catholic seriousness. Kevin's mother wrote that she didn't agree. Kevin ended up attending public school, so he guessed his mother won that argument.

Kevin's mother's entry on Monday, February 9, 2015, said that Kevin had called her that afternoon. He remembered calling her. It was the first full day of research in the Gorge. He and Kate had just finished eating, and Kevin had decided to phone, thinking that he might get too caught up in the research that he would forget to call his mother regularly. She wrote that Kevin had sounded excited and spoke about some plant that you could only find in the Red River Gorge. His mother wrote that she wished Kevin would show the same excitement for his Soul but had refrained from telling Kevin this.

Kevin recalled that his mother had been quiet on

the phone for the majority of that conversation. She didn't ask him about the research but did ask him if he was going to find a church out there to go to. The question had caught him off guard. His mother hadn't really asked him about his church attendance since his undergraduate days.

Kevin told her that he thought she knew that he didn't attend church and added, quickly, that this was because he didn't have the time. He remembered feeling like chickenshit for not leaving it as it should be, that he didn't attend church or believe in all that superstitious mumbo jumbo either.

Kevin's mother had sensed it though and wrote that she felt a stab of remorse and another of shame. She wrote that the phone call ended shortly thereafter, and she prayed for Kevin's Soul. She wrote that she wished she could open Kevin's eyes to the Light of the Lord.

Kevin shuddered; his stomach soured. He left one piece of toast uneaten and tossed it into the garbage. He made himself another cup of bitter black coffee.

****

On Wednesday, February 25, 2015, his mother wrote that Jeremiah Jeffrey had phoned her that afternoon.

His voice, usually quiet and low, danced up and down like he was chanting or singing a song, not having a conversation. He said that he had consulted the leaves and that God Almighty had lined up a plan and that he knew his course of action. Jeremiah Jeffrey asked me if I was ready, and I told him I was. He said that Kevin's Salvation was on course to be achieved before Christ's Second Coming.

****

Monday, March 2, 2015: Jeremiah Jeffrey called today, said the Second Advent was imminent. He said he'd read the leaves, and the leaves told him to warn the people to get right with God. That He was coming. Soon. I felt scared for Kevin and asked if he was going to be ready, pure, in time.

Jeremiah Jeffrey was quiet for a minute, and I thought I could hear scratching or some such noise from his end, then he said that Kevin was going to have to make the choice himself. I yelled that I thought he said he could save his Soul and that's what all of this business was about, and Jeremiah Jeffrey said that God had control of the matter now. He asked me to put my trust in the Good Lord.

I was so tore up after that call I went and talked to Pastor C about my fear for Kevin's Soul some more. I haven't told him about Jeremiah Jeffrey, and he hasn't asked about it since giving me the flyer. Pastor C told me to focus on the good things that I can remember teaching Kevin and to have faith that he will come around and accept the Light in due time.

****

"Welcome, Trooper Terry," JJ Conn said.

He was sitting with Abigail on his lap, her mouth taped shut, her eyes wide and terrified, snot streaking down her little nose. Francine was tied to a chair at the head of the table, her mouth also taped shut, her eyes, wild and frenzied.

"Police," Stewart shouted from the front.

"Hold on," Terry called back. "Don't move, Stewart."

"I told you to come alone," Conn said.

"I can't drive," Terry said. "I can barely see

straight, you son of a bitch."

He couldn't see the man's hands. They were carefully hidden behind Abi's small, shaking frame.

"Let her go," Terry said.

JJ Conn smiled. It was a sickening sight.

"Terry, what's going on?" Stewart called. "Is he back there?"

The large pale man slowly slid the blade of a long, curved knife out from behind Abigail. He held it just below her chin.

Terry felt like puking. His body shook and fresh sweat dripped. He felt it pool between the trigger and the skin of his finger. He kept the flashlight trained on the man holding his daughter but lowered the gun, unsure and frightened.

"Let her go, Conn."

"I need something from you, Trooper Terry," JJ Conn said. "I need you to call off your little search. I need a little breathing room."

He flicked the knife against Abigail's skin. A motion akin to shaving. The noise loud and carrying in the quiet darkness.

Terry swallowed a mouthful of vomit. "That's not possible."

"With God, all things are possible."

Terry watched the man slowly pull her closer, no space between the blade and Abi's bare throat.

"I just need a few hours head start. I don't expect you to be able to call the hounds of Hell off completely. God's work is always persecuted."

"Terry, what the fuck is going on back there?" Stewart shouted. "Talk to me, goddamn it."

"You crazy son of a bitch," Terry said. "You'll fry

for this."

The radio crackled to life on Terry's belt. He recognized Stewart's hushed voice. He slowly moved the hand holding the gun down to the radio and, using the outside of his hand, turned the volume to zero.

"Beloved, do not be surprised at the fiery trial when it comes upon you to test you, as though something strange were happening to you. But rejoice insofar as you share Christ's sufferings..." JJ Conn pushed the blade into Abi's throat, a thin trickle of blood flowed, the muffled hurt of her voice like needles in Terry's heart. "...that you may also rejoice and be glad when his glory is revealed. If you are insulted for the name of Christ, you are blessed, because the Spirit of glory and of God rests upon you."

Francine violently jerked in the chair, her screaming muffled by the tape.

It was distraction enough.

JJ Conn turned his neck toward Francine, and Abi slid away from the man's body, all in one motion.

Terry didn't think. He caught his breath, raised the gun, and fired.

****

Thursday, March 12, 2015: Jeremiah Jeffrey woke me in the dead of night. He was standing there in the door of my bedroom, telling me to wake up in his soft voice. I thought I was dreaming at first; then I thought something must be wrong. Why was Jeremiah Jeffrey in my house? How did he keep getting in? I asked him if Kevin was ok, and he just said to wake up and follow him.

I pulled on my robe and followed him into the living room. He had lit the candle on the coffee table and had my Bible laying there beside it, but there was another Bible on the table, too, an old, worn black one with a dark red cross on the cover. I reached to turn on the light, but he told me to stop. He told me to sit down on the couch beside him.

I sat down and he took up his Bible and opened it all the way to the back, where there was a little pouch cut into the thick leather. Jeremiah Jeffrey slid several fingers into the slit, and they came back with a thin leaf. He held it up for me to examine. He said it was called White-Sight. He said the long and short of it was the fact that God had left it for the Anointed to use in prophesy. He said God left messages in the verses that could only be seen through leaf reading. He handed me the leaf and told me to make any preparations I needed to "for the end was near at hand."

Kevin flung his mother's Bible open and moved all the pages to the front cover. There was no pouch in his mother's Bible and no *Solidago albopilosa* leaves or flower heads. Kevin marked his page in his mother's diary with one hand and flipped to the back.

There it sat. Spatula-shaped, crushed, and dried but unmistakably covered in tiny white hairs, a leaf from the white-haired goldenrod. White-Sight.

Kevin lifted the leaf and set it down gently in the palm of his hand. He could barely feel it; it was so light. He picked it back up by its stem and twirled it around, making one full revolution.

Kevin couldn't help himself. He scoffed at the mere notion of it working, but there he was scooting the diary out of the way and pulling the Bible in front of him.

"I'm losing my goddamned mind." Kevin laughed

to himself.

He turned the pages into the New Testament and the Book of Luke. He turned to chapter eight and verse seventeen.

Kevin read it out loud again, "For nothing is hidden that will not be made manifest, nor is anything secret that will not be known and come to light."

Kevin turned his palm over and the dry leaf dropped onto the thin Bible pages unceremoniously. Kevin placed his fingertips lightly on the leaf, his planchette, and moved the leaf over the text of Luke 8:17, his Ouija board. Kevin squinted his eyes and dropped his head over the leaf, trying to make something out of it. All he saw were the small white hairs and the top of the dried leaf.

"You died for nothing, my friend," Kevin said to the leaf.

He returned the leaf to its place in the back of his mother's diary, closed the Bible, and slid it to the far side of the table.

****

Monday, March 16, 2015: Jeremiah Jeffrey called today. Before he could say anything, I asked him how the leaf worked, the White-Sight. He hesitated a moment, then told me that, if I didn't see nothing, it didn't mean it doesn't work. Jeremiah Jeffrey said that God connects with those nearest to Him and he didn't find it unusual that I couldn't read the leaf.

Then he asked me if I'd been baptized. I told him, of course, I had. He asked if it had been a living water baptism, if I had been baptized in one of the Good Lord's streams or lakes. I hadn't. I asked him if this mattered, and he jeered me with such a laugh and in that soft voice of his, too!

Jeremiah Jeffrey told me that I needed to get myself right with God because He was coming soon. He told me that Kevin was going to have a heart to heart with God Almighty in the very near future. Like he could read my mind, he said that he wasn't gonna hurt Kevin. I lied and told him that I wasn't thinking he would.

Then he told me to gather what resolve I could find because the trials and tribulations of a wayward Soul were not a thing to trifle with. The fire is hot, and it'll rain down from both above and below 'fore this one's over, he said.

****

He screamed her name, over and over and over again, in the swirling darkness. He wasn't sure if it was the slickness of his hands or the recoil of the shot, but Terry dropped the flashlight. It'd hit the floor and blinked out, returning the kitchen into a stygian, brooding blackness.

Terry went lumbering on unsteady feet into the table, groping with his free left hand for his daughter, the right still holding the gun.

"Where are you?" he called. "I can't see you, baby. Where are you?"

He found something wet and hot. He was sure he was going to throw up.

"Abigail? Abi? Is that you?"

He slapped at the unmoving object, felt cloth and flesh and wetness. A smell, vaguely metallic, iron and copper, made his stomach clench tighter.

A little flicker of movement and Terry was pulled away. He heard his gun clatter down out of his hand, onto the hardwood.

"I'm right here, Daddy," a little voice cried. "I'm right here."

Oh, God.

Terry let himself be led away by two surprisingly strong hands. They found his and pulled him down to his knees. Then he was enveloped by the sound of her sobs, her gasps of relief and terror and confusion, her understanding that Daddy was there now.

"Shh," he told her. "Hush, now. It's ok."

"Terry," Stewart yelled, the light of his flashlight piercing the darkness. "Terry."

In the light of Stewart's flashlight, Terry finally saw his daughter's tear-stained face, the flap of tape hanging from her cracked and bleeding lips, a dark trickle at her throat, and wrapped his arms around her.

****

When he could see through the tears and swimming dark currents of light and movement, Terry saw the slumped shape of Jeremiah Jeffrey Conn in the glow of Stewart's shaky light. His eyes were closed, his mouth open, a thin strand of spit and blood hanging. He could've been sleeping, meditating, praying.

The man's trunk, neck, and face were bloodied, splatters of red and black, a growing stain, but after several long moments, Terry could just make out the shallow rise and fall of the pale man's chest.

Sirens screamed out into the night.

Flashes of blue grew in intensity.

Terry closed his eyes and held his daughter.

****

Sunday, March 22, 2015: He was here when I got back from church. Jeremiah Jeffrey was sitting on the front porch, just reading his red cross Bible. He smiled and looked me full in the face when I came up the walk. I hate to say it, but I was scared there at first. I'd been so confused after I talked with him on the phone last week, but he straightened things out for me today. Everything is in its right place.

He said he came down because he wanted to ensure my Soul was pure. I got sorta offended at first, but he sat me down on the old church pew there on the porch and told me how Jesus was baptized by John the Baptist in the river Jordan. He said, though I'd been "baptized," it wasn't as the Lord intended. Baptism wasn't about convenience; it was about being washed clean of your sins and becoming Born Again.

He said he wanted to take me around back, down the hill to the Nolin River, and give me a proper baptism. He reached out and held my hands and spoke so softly.

Now, I can't lie and say I see any real difference between the two. I think being born again, if you really mean it, in a tub or a muddy ol' river, is still being Born Again. Po-tate-oh; Po-taut-oh. But I wanted to show him ~~how committed I was~~ how committed I am.

I told him that I was willing to do whatever it takes.

As his mother, I have to do whatever I can do, give anything and everything, absolutely whatever it takes, to get Kevin right with God. Jeremiah Jeffrey said this was paramount for the conversion, so I agreed.

I am Saved, again.

The last page of his mother's diary was empty, save the leaf of the white-haired goldenrod and, in red ink, *Jeremiah 51:40* written in the exact center of the page.

Kevin reached across the table and brought his

mother's Bible before him again. He located the Book of Jeremiah, then chapter fifty-one and finally verse forty, and read, "I will bring them down like lambs to the slaughter, like rams and goats."

A word about the author...

A.S. Coomer is a writer, musician, artist, taco fanatic, and perpetual rain dog. Novels include: *Rush's Deal* (Hammer & Anvil Books/Lit Fest Press), *The Fetishists* (Grindhouse Press), *The Devil's Gospel* (The Wild Rose Press), and *Shining the Light* (Atlatl Press). He runs Lost, Long Gone, Forgotten Records, a "record label" for poetry.

www.ascoomer.com

www.ingramcontent.com/pod-product-compliance
Lightning Source LLC
Chambersburg PA
CBHW070453260626
47161CB00004B/1281